THE TRUCE

THE TRUCE

by *Mario Benedetti*

TRANSLATED FROM THE SPANISH BY BENJAMIN GRAHAM

HARPER & ROW, PUBLISHERS

NEW YORK, EVANSTON, AND LONDON

16667

This book was originally published
in Uruguay under the title *La Tregua*.

FIRST U.S. EDITION 1969

LIBRARY OF CONGRESS CATALOG CARD NUMBER: 76-88642

ESBPC   5.95   10/17/69

Mi mano derecha es una golondrina
Mi mano izquierda es un ciprés
Mi cabeza por delante es un señor vivo
Y por detrás es un señor muerto.

—VICENTE HUIDOBRO

THE TRUCE

In just six months and twenty-eight days I'll be all set for my retirement. It must be at least five years that I've been making this daily calculation. Do I really need leisure that much? I tell myself, "No, it isn't leisure that I need but the right to work at what I want." For example? The garden, maybe. That's a good thing as an active way of resting on Sundays, as a countermeasure for a sedentary life, and even as a secret defense against my guaranteed arthritis. But I'm afraid that I couldn't take it as a daily dose. The same with the guitar. I think I'd like it. But it would be pretty tough to begin picking out notes at the age of forty-nine. Writing? Perhaps I wouldn't do too badly at that; at least, people usually enjoy my letters. But then what? I imagine some critic's note on "the values that may be expected from this new author who is flirting with his fifties," and the mere possibility disgusts me. Granted that I feel myself, even today, naïve and immature (i.e., with only the defects of youth and with none of its virtues); that doesn't mean that I have the right to make an exhibition of this immaturity. I had an old-maid cousin who, when she made some dessert or other, would show it to everybody with a melancholy and childish smile, which had remained fixed on her lips from the time that she wished to make a good impression on her motorcycling fiancé who was later killed on one of our many "Death Curves." She dressed correctly, in a manner generally suitable for her fifty-three years; in that and other things she was discreet and well-balanced; but that smile, by contrast, demanded an accompaniment of the fresh lips, the rosy skin and the well-turned legs of a twenty-year-old. It was a pathetic gesture, nothing more, a gesture that never went so far as to appear ridiculous, because one could see goodness as well on her face. How many words, just to say that I don't want to appear pathetic.

FRIDAY, FEBRUARY **15**

To do reasonably good work in the office I have to keep myself from thinking that my retirement is relatively close. Otherwise my fingers get stiff and the round-hand letters in which I write the account headings turn out broken and without elegance. Round hand is one of my best credits as an employee. Furthermore, I must confess, I get pleasure out of the form of certain letters, such as capital *M* and small *b*, in which I have permitted myself one or two innovations. What I dislike the least is the mechanical, routine part of my work: making an entry once again that I have put together thousands of times; casting a trial balance and finding that all is in order, and there is no difference to ferret out. This type of work doesn't tire me, because it permits me to think about other things, and even (why shouldn't I say that to myself?) to dream. It's as if I were divided into two beings, different, contradictory, independent. One who knows his work by heart, who is completely master of its ins and outs, who is always sure of what he's doing; the other dreamy and

[2]

feverish, full of frustrated passion, a sad chap who, none-theless, had, has and will have a call to joy; an absent-minded fellow who has no concern with where his pen is running or what things are being written by that blue ink which will turn black in eight months.

In my work the insupportable part is not the routine; it is the new problem, the unexpected request from that phantasmagoric Management which hides itself behind announcements, instructions and rewards. It's the urgency with which it demands certain information, or an analysis of an account, or a forecast of the cash balance. In such a case, since it's a question of something more than routine, my two halves have to work as one. I can no longer think about what I prefer, and fatigue takes its place in my back and the nape of my neck, like a porous plaster. What do I care about the approximate profit from the account *Pernos de Piston* in the second half of the fiscal year before last? What do I care about the most practicable way of effecting a decrease in General Expenses?

Today was a happy day; nothing but routine.

MONDAY, FEBRUARY 18

None of my three children resembles me. In the first place they all have more energy than I, and are not accustomed to being in doubt. Esteban is the least sociable. I still don't know whom he is angry at, but he surely gives the appearance of an angry man. I believe he respects me, but I'm never positive. Jaime is perhaps my favorite, even though we practically never understand one another. He seems to me to be sensitive and intelligent, but he doesn't appear fundamentally honest. It is evident that a barrier exists between him and me. At times I believe he hates me, at times that he admires me. Blanca has at least something in common with me; she too is a sad one with a call to joyfulness. However, she is too jealous of her private life, unbending, unwilling to share her most difficult problems with me. It is she who spends the most time at home, and thus she feels somewhat a slave of our disorder, our diets, our dirty clothes. Her relations with her brothers at times border on the hysterical, but she knows how to master herself and she even knows how to master them. Perhaps at bottom they love each other, though this kind of love between siblings carries its customary quota of mutual exasperation. No, they don't resemble me. Not even physically. Esteban and Blanca have Isabel's eyes. Jaime inherited her forehead and mouth. What would Isabel think if she could see them today, preoccupied, active, grown up? I have a better question: What would I think today if I could see Isabel? Death is a boring experience for those who remain, *especially* for those who remain. I ought to feel proud about having been left a widower with three children and having made out OK. But I don't feel proud, only tired. Pride is for when one is twenty or thirty. To get by all right with my children was an obligation, the only way to keep society from looking me up and down and giving me that inexorable glance reserved by it for cruel and inhuman parents. There was nothing else I could do, and so I got by. But all that was too much of an obligation to permit me to feel happy about it.

TUESDAY, FEBRUARY **19**

At 4 P.M. I suddenly felt intolerably empty. I had to change from my office coat and tell the personnel department that I must go over to the bank to arrange some matter of foreign exchange. I was lying. What I couldn't endure any longer was that wall in front of my desk, that terrible wall all taken up by that enormous calendar with February consecrated to Goya. What is Goya doing in this old established firm that imports auto replacement parts? I don't know what would have happened if I had kept on looking at the calendar like an imbecile. Perhaps I would have yelled, or begun one of my customary series of allergic sneezes, or perhaps merely buried myself in the neat pages of *Mayor* magazine. For I've already learned that my states of pre-outbreak don't always lead to an actual seizure. At times they end in humiliation, in an acceptance, as without remedy, of the circumstances and their various and aggravating pressures. However, I like to convince myself that I shouldn't allow these attacks, that I must control them completely on pain of losing my mental balance. So I walk out, as I went out today, in a desperate search for free air, for the horizon, for who knows how many other things. Agreed, at times I don't reach the horizon, and I settle for a place near the window of a café, where I can note the passing of some shapely legs.

I'm convinced that the city is different during office hours. I know the Montevideo of men on a schedule, of those who arrive at eight-thirty and leave at twelve, who return at two-thirty and leave for the day at seven, with those tight and sweaty faces, with those hurried and stumbling steps. I'm well acquainted with all that. But it's the other city, the one of fresh little frails who go out in the middle of the afternoon newly bathed, perfumed, full of superiority, optimism and bright remarks; the city of mamas' boys who wake up at noon, and at 6 P.M. still haven't a spot on the white collars of their imported knit shirts; the city of the old men who take the bus as far as the customhouse and then return without getting out, this modest diversion thus reduced to merely the comforted glance with which they come back to the old city of their homesick memories; the city of the young mothers who never go out at night but who enter the cinema at half-past three with guilty faces; the city of nurses who say bad things about their madams while flies are eating up their charges; finally, the city of retired people and bores of various sorts, who think they will gain heaven by giving crumbs to the pigeons in the plaza—those are the ones I don't know, for the present at least. They are installed all too comfortably in their own lives, while I go crazy in front of a calendar with its February consecrated to Goya.

FRIDAY, FEBRUARY 22

When I retire I think I won't continue this diary, because then, no doubt, fewer things will happen to me than now, and I won't be able to stand feeling myself so useless and at the same time leaving a written account of this futility. When I retire, furthermore, the best thing would be to abandon myself to my leisure, to a sort of compensatory drowsiness, in order that my nerves, muscles and energy might relax a bit and accustom themselves to dying. But no. There are moments when I catch and hold on to the luxurious hope that my leisure will be something full and rich, the last opportunity to meet myself. If so, that would really be worth the trouble of describing it.

Today I lunched alone in the Center. When I was going down Mercedes Street I passed a fellow in a reddish-brown suit. He gave me a slight nod. I must have looked at him inquisitively, for the man stopped and after some hesitation offered me his hand. His face was not unfamiliar. It was a bit like a caricature of someone whom I had known, in times past at least. I shook hands with him, murmuring excuses and confessing my perplexity in one way or another. "Martín Santomé?" he asked, his smile showing a pretty bad set of teeth. "Yes, I am Martín Santomé," but my embarrassment kept growing. "Don't you remember Brandzen Street?" Yes, but not very well. That was about thirty years ago, and I'm not famous for my memory. I did live on Brandzen Street before my marriage, but even if they beat me for it I couldn't say how the front of our house looked, how many balconies it had, who lived next door to me. "And the café on Defensa Street?" Now at last the cloud was dissipated a little and I saw for a moment the Galician Álvarez with his broad-belted stomach. "Of course, of course!" I exclaimed, a light dawning. "Good; and I'm Mario Vignale." Mario Vignale? I just didn't remember him, I swear I didn't remember him. But I hadn't the courage to confess it. The chap appeared so excited about this meeting. I told him he would have to excuse me, that I had no memory at all for faces, that only last week I had met a cousin and hadn't recognized him (lie). Naturally, I had to take a cup of coffee with him, so that ruined my Saturday nap. It used up two hours and a quarter. He insisted on recalling all sorts of details to convince me that

[7]

he had participated in my life. "I remember even the squash omelets your old woman used to make. Sensational. I used to come always at eleven-thirty, to see if she would invite me to eat with you." And he let out a tremendous guffaw. "Always?" I asked him, still suspicious. That question shamed him a bit. "Well, let's say it was three or four times." So how much truth was there in all he was saying? "And your mother, is she OK?" "She died fifteen years ago." "Too bad!" "And your old man?" "He died two years ago in Tacuarembó. We were staying at the house of my Aunt Leonor." "She must be pretty old." Sure, she had to be pretty old. My God, what a nuisance! Only then did he put the most logical question: "Say, did you marry Isabel after all?" "Yes, and I have three children," I answered, shortening the route. He has five. What luck. "And how is Isabel? Still pretty?" "She died," I said, putting on the most inscrutable expression in my repertory. The words sounded like a gun going off, and he, fortunately, was disconcerted. He hurried to finish his third cup of coffee and immediately looked at his watch. There is a kind of automatic reflex by which one speaks of death and immediately looks at one's watch.

SUNDAY, FEBRUARY 24

There's really no reason for it, but the interview with Vignale left me with an obsession: to remember Isabel. Still, it's not a matter of following her image through familiar anecdotes, or photographs, or one or another feature of Esteban or Blanca. I know all her characteristics, but I don't want to know them at second hand. I want rather to remember them directly, to see them before me in every detail as I am now seeing my face in the mirror. And I'm not succeeding. I know that she had black hair, but I can't see her black hair. I know that she had green eyes, but I can't feel her glance resting on me.

I rarely spend time with my children. Our schedules don't often coincide and our plans and interests even less. They are correct with me, but since they are also tremendously reserved, their correct behavior seems merely the accomplishment of a duty. Esteban, for example, always refrains from arguing about any of my opinions. Is it simply the distance of a generation that separates us, or could I myself do something more to communicate with them? In general I find them skeptical rather than completely negative, and more withdrawn than I was at their age.

Today we had dinner together. Probably it's been about two months since we were all present at a family meal. I asked, as a joke, what special event we were celebrating, but there was no echo. Blanca looked at me and smiled, as if to let me know that she understood my good intentions, but no more. I set myself to observing what were the few interruptions of the religious silence. Jaime said that the soup was tasteless. "You have the salt there, four inches from your right hand," answered Blanca, and added sarcastically, "Do you want me to pass it to you?" The soup needed salt, sure enough, but why the fuss? Esteban informed us that beginning next week our rent will go up eighty pesos. Since we all contribute to the cost, that's not so serious. Jaime began to read the newspaper. I consider it impolite for people to read when they eat with their family. I said so. Jaime put the paper down, but it was the same as if he had gone on reading, for he continued boorish and ill-humored.

I related my meeting with Vignale, trying to make it appear as ridiculous as possible to bring some animation to our dinner. But Jaime asked, "Which Vignale is it?" "Mario Vignale." "A partly bald fellow with a mustache?" "Right." "I know him. Some guy. He's a pal of Ferreira and a stupid brute." At bottom I was glad to hear that Vignale was a sort of swine, for then I need have no scruples about getting rid of him. But Blanca asked, "So he remembered Mother?" It seemed to me that Jaime was going to say something. I believe his lips moved, but he remained silent. "Lucky for him," added Blanca. "I don't remember her." "I do," said Esteban. How would he remember? Like me, with memories of memories, or directly, as someone sees his own face in the mirror? Would it be possible that he, who was only four years old then, could hold on to her image, while I, on the other hand, who carry so many, many nights impressed on my memory, am still left with nothing of *her*? We used to make love in the dark. That's the reason. I'm sure that's the reason. I keep a tactile memory of those nights, and that memory is direct enough. But what about the days? During the days, of course, I could see her. But I used to come home tired out, full of problems, perhaps boiling mad at the injustice of that week, or that month.

At times we worked on our accounts. They never came out right. But we were looking too much at the numbers, the additions, the subtractions, and we didn't have time to look at each other. Where she is now, if she is anywhere, what memory would she have of me? But at bottom, does memory have any importance? "At times I feel unlucky, just because I don't know what I've been missing," murmured Blanca, while she divided up the peaches in syrup. We each got three and a half.

Today seven new employees came into the office: four men and three women. Their faces were glistening with a sort of fear, and from time to time they directed a glance of respectful envy at the veterans. I was allotted two young fellows (one eighteen, the other twenty-two) and a girl of twenty-four. So now I'm really a boss. I've got no less than six workers under my orders. And, for the first time, a woman. I always found them unreliable at figures. Besides, another drawback: during their periods, and even a short time before, if normally they're intelligent they become rather stupid; if normally they're a bit stupid they become completely imbecile. The new men who are coming in don't look bad. The eighteen-year-old is the one I like least. He has a face without strength, too delicate, and a look that's evasive when it isn't frowning. The other's hair is never combed, but he has a sympathetic aspect and (for now, at least) an evident desire to work. The girl doesn't seem overeager to work, but at least she understands what one explains to her; furthermore, she has a broad forehead and a large mouth, two traits that in general impress me. The three are named Alfred Santini, Rodolpho Sierra and Laura Avellaneda. I'll give the merchandise inventories to the men and the auxiliary ledger to her.

THURSDAY, FEBRUARY 28

Tonight I conversed with a Blanca almost unknown to me. We were alone after dinner. I was reading the paper and she was playing solitaire. Suddenly she sat motionless, with a card in the air, and she looked both lost in thought and very sad. I watched for some moments; then I asked her what she was thinking about. At that she seemed to wake up, directed a desolate glance at me and, unable to contain herself, she hid her head in her hands, as if she wanted no profane glance to see her weeping. When a woman cries before my eyes I become helpless, and awkward to boot. I go desperate, not knowing how to fix things. This time I followed a natural impulse; I got up, went over to her and began to caress her head, without saying a word. Little by little she calmed down, and the fits of weeping became less frequent. When at last she dropped her hands, I employed the unused half of my handkerchief to dry her eyes and wipe her nose. At that instant she didn't look like a woman of twenty-three, but rather like a little girl momentarily unhappy because she had broken a doll or because we didn't take her to the zoo. I asked her if she was unhappy, and she answered yes. I asked her why and she said she didn't know. I wasn't too surprised. I too feel miserable at times without a concrete reason. But against my own experience I said, "Oh, there's something wrong. You don't cry for no reason." Then she began to talk at full speed, urged on by a sudden desire to be frank: "I have the horrible feeling that time is passing and I'm not accomplishing anything, that nothing is happening to me down to my very roots. I look at Esteban and at Jaime and I'm sure they're miserable too. Sometimes—don't get angry, Papá—I look at you also and I think I wouldn't like to reach fifty years and possess your temperament and your superficial air of balance, because quite simply I find them flat and wasted away. I feel I've got a lot of energy, but I don't know how to use it, I don't know what to do with it. I believe you've resigned yourself to being dull, and that's horrible, because I know that you're not dull. At least you didn't use to be." I replied (what else could I say?) that she was right, that she should do everything possible to get away from us, from our routine, that I was very pleased to hear her give this nonconformist cry, that I seemed to be hearing a cry of my own that went back many years. Then she smiled, said I was very kind, and she flung her arms around my neck, as she used to do. She's still a little girl.

FRIDAY, MARCH 1

The general manager called in the five chiefs of section. During three-quarters of an hour he lectured us about the low efficiency of the staff. He said that the board of directors had sent him a criticism to this effect; and that in the future he wasn't disposed to allow that because of our sloth (how he liked to mouth the word "sloth") his position should be impaired without reason. Therefore, from now on . . . etc., etc.

What did they call "low output of the staff"? I can say, at least, that my people work. And not only the newcomers, but the old ones as well. Sure, Méndez reads crime stories which he sets up skillfully in the middle drawer of his desk, while his right hand holds a pen always ready for the possible entry of some higher-up. Sure, Muñoz takes advantage of his trips to Profit Development to steal from the business twenty minutes of leisure in front of a glass of beer. Sure, Robledo when he goes to the toilet (exactly at ten-fifteen) carries under his smock the color supplement or the sports section. But it's also certain that the work is always up to date, and in the hours of pressure, when the aerial message box from the Cashier's Department keeps traveling without a pause, filled with slips, they all become enthusiastic and work with a real team spirit. In his limited specialty each is an expert, and I can be fully confident that things are being done right.

In reality I know very well where the manager's outburst was directed. Deliveries works without any drive, and besides, it does its job badly. We all knew today that the harangue was delivered for Suárez; but then why did he call us all in? What right has Suárez to make us share a blame that belongs to him alone? Is it because the manager knows, as all of us do, that Suárez sleeps with the president's daughter? She's not a bad-looker, that Lidia Valverde.

SATURDAY, MARCH 2

Last night, after thirty years, I dreamed again of my hooded men. When I was four years old, or possibly less, eating was a nightmare. It was then my grandmother invented a really original method to make me swallow my mashed potatoes without making too much trouble. She put on an enormous raincoat of my uncle's, turned up the hood and added black spectacles. With that frightening aspect, she came to knock at my window. The servant, my mother and one of my aunts then chorused, "Here's Don Policarpo!" Don Policarpo was a sort of monster who beat up children who wouldn't eat. Nailed down as I was by my own terror, what was left of my strength succeeded in moving my jaws at incredible speed and in finishing the tasteless and overabundant puree. That was a convenient arrangement for everybody. Threatening me with Don Policarpo was equivalent to pressing a magic button. In the end they had converted it into a famous diversion. When a visitor would arrive they dragged him to my room so he could witness the amusing details of my panic. It's strange how people at times can succeed in being so innocently cruel. For, in addition to my fright, my nights—ah! my nights—were filled with silent hooded men, a rare species of Policarpo, who always had their backs turned and were surrounded by a thick fog. They invariably appeared in a line, as if waiting their turn to enter into my fear. They never said a word, but they moved heavily, with a kind of intermittent sway, dragging their dark jackets, all similar, into which my uncle's raincoat had been transformed. It was curious: in my dream I felt less horror than in the reality. And, as the years passed, my fear was converted into fascination. With that absorbed glance we seem able to maintain beneath our dreaming eyelids, I watched the recurrent scene as if hypnotized. At times, dreaming some other dream, I was obscurely conscious that I would have preferred to dream my Policarpos. And one night they came for the last time. They formed their line, they swayed, they kept silent and, as was customary, they vanished. During many years I slept with a constant feeling of lack, with an almost sick sensation of waiting. At times I went to sleep determined to meet them again, but I succeeded only in creating the fog and, on rare occasions, in feeling the palpitations of my ancient fear. Only that. Afterward I gradually lost even that hope, and insensibly arrived at the period when I began to tell the simple structure of that dream to strangers. I even came to forget it. Until last night. Last night, when I was in the very center of a dream more vulgar than sinful, the figures became smudged, the fog appeared, and in the midst of the fog my Policarpos. I know that I felt unspeakably happy and horrified. So, if I make an effort, I can still reconstruct something of that emotion. The Policarpos, the shapeless, eternal, harmless Policarpos of my childhood, swayed, swayed again, and, suddenly, did something entirely unexpected. For the first time they turned around, just for a moment, and every one of them had the face of my grandmother.

TUESDAY, MARCH 12

It's good to have an intelligent employee. Today, to try out Avellaneda, I explained to her at one go all about controls. While I was talking she took notes. When I finished she said, "Look, sir, I think I understood it well enough, but I have doubts about some points." Méndez, who took care of that matter before her, needed no less than four years to dissipate *his* doubts. Afterward I set her to work at the table at my right. From time to time I glanced at her. She has pretty legs. Still, she doesn't work automatically, so she gets tired. Furthermore she is fidgety and nervous. I think my position as boss inhibits her. (Poor beginner!) When she says "Señor Santomé" she always blinks. She isn't a beauty, but she smiles passably. A little something is better than nothing.

WEDNESDAY, MARCH 13

This afternoon, when I came home from downtown, Jaime and Esteban were shouting in the kitchen. I was able to hear Esteban saying something about "your rotten friends." As soon as they heard my steps they stopped yelling, and tried to converse naturally. But Jaime kept his lips pressed together, and Esteban's eyes were ablaze.

"What is going on?" I asked. Jaime shrugged his shoulders, and the other said, "None of your business." How I wanted to give him a good sock in the mouth. That is my son, that hard face that nothing will ever soften. None of my business! I went to the icebox and took out a bottle of milk and the butter. I felt defeated and humiliated. It wasn't possible that he could say to me "None of your business" and that I should remain so quiet, doing nothing, saying nothing. I poured myself a large glass. He can't be allowed to shout at me in the tone I should be using with him but which I didn't use. "None of your business, none of your business." Every swallow of milk I took hurt my temples. Suddenly I turned around and took him by the arm. "More respect for your father, do you understand? More respect!" It was idiotic to say that now when the moment had already passed. His arm was tense and hard as if all at once it had been turned to steel or lead. The back of my neck hurt me when I raised my head to look him in the eyes. That was the least I could do. No, he wasn't scared. He simply shook his arm until he got it loose, moved his nostrils and said, "When will you grow up?" then he went out, slamming the door. I couldn't have had a very tranquil expression when I turned to face Jaime. He was leaning against the wall. He smiled quite naturally and remarked only, "What bad blood, bad blood." It is incredible, but at that moment I felt that my anger was melting. "Still, he is your brother," I said, without conviction. "Let him be," he answered. "At this point there is nothing any of us can do."

FRIDAY, MARCH 15

Mario Vignale came to see me at the office. He wants me to come to his house next week. He says he has found old photos of all of us. The big fool didn't bring them with him. Naturally, they were the bait for my acceptance. So I accepted. Who isn't attracted by his own past?

SATURDAY, MARCH 16

This morning the new man, Santini, tried to confess himself to me. I don't know what my face has that always invites confidences. They look at me, they smile at me, some go as far as making the grimace that precedes a sob. Then they dedicate themselves to opening their hearts. And frankly there are hearts that don't interest me. It is incredible, the convenient shamelessness, the tone of mystery, that some characters secrete about themselves. "Because, do you know, sir, I am an orphan," he said, as he came in, to draw my pity. "Pleased to meet you; and I am a widower," I answered with a ritual gesture intended to counter his gambit. But my widowerhood moved him much less than his orphanhood. "I have a little sister, you know." While he spoke, standing next to my desk, he kept tapping his soft and slender fingers against the cover of my journal. "Can't you keep that hand quiet?" I barked at him; but he smiled sweetly before obeying. He wore a bracelet of gold with a little medal on his wrist. "My little sister is seventeen years old, you know." "You know" is a sort of tic. "You don't say! And is she all right?" That was my last defense before the weak dikes of his scruples would give way and I would find myself up to my neck in his intimate life. "You don't take me seriously," he said, compressing his lips; and he went back to his table, much offended. He didn't work too rapidly. He was two hours late with the résumé of February.

If I ever commit suicide it will be on Sunday. It is the most insipid and the most discouraging day of the week. I wanted to stay in my room until late, at least until nine or ten, but at six-thirty I woke up and then I couldn't close my eyes. At times I think of what I'll do when all my life will be Sunday. Who knows, perhaps I'll accustom myself to waking up at ten o'clock. I went to eat lunch at the Center, because the children had gone away for the weekend, each on his own. I ate alone. I didn't even have the energy to start up with the waiter the simple, ritual exchange of opinions about the heat and the tourists. Two tables away there was another solitary diner. He was frowning, and he cut up his rolls with sharp movements of his knife. I looked at him two or three times, and on one occasion my glance crossed his. It seemed to me that there was hatred on his side. What look was there for him in my eyes? It must be a general rule that solitary people don't sympathize. Or could it be simply that the two of us were antipathetic?

I returned home, took my siesta and woke up feeling heavy and in bad humor. I drank some maté and was angry because it tasted bitter. Then I dressed and went back downtown. That time I went into a café. I got a table next to the window. In the space of an hour and a quarter there passed by exactly thirty-five women of interest. For my entertainment I made a count of what I liked best in each of them. I marked it on the paper napkin. This is the result: Of two, I liked the face; of four, the hair; of eight, the legs; of fifteen, the behind. A great victory for the behinds.

Last night Esteban came in at midnight, Jaime at twelve-thirty and Blanca at one-thirty. I heard each of them, and picked up each noise, each step, each vulgar word the boys muttered. I think that Jaime returned a little drunk. At least, he stumbled against the furniture and left the tap of the washbasin open for about a half hour. However, the gross words were from Esteban, who never drinks. When Blanca came in, Esteban said something to her from his room, and she told him to mind his own business. After that, silence. Three hours of silence. Insomnia is the plague of my weekends. When I retire shall I never sleep?

This morning I spoke to Blanca alone. I told her I didn't like her coming home at such hours. She wasn't insolent in any way that would merit a reprimand. But, in any case, this is our duty, the duty of a father and mother. I have to be both at once, and I believe I am neither. I felt I was going too far when I heard myself saying in a warning tone, "What were you doing? Where were you?" Then she, while I spread butter on my toast, answered, "Why do you feel obliged to hurt yourself? There are two things we can be sure about: We love each other, and I am not doing anything wrong." I was put to rout. However, I added, if for no more than to save appearances, "It all depends on what you understand by 'wrong.' "

I worked all the afternoon with Avellaneda, in search of a discrepancy. The most boring kind that exists.

Seven cents. But in truth it was made up of two contrary differences, one of eighteen cents and the other of twenty-five. But the poor girl didn't really get the hang of it. In a completely automatic job like this she gets tired as quickly as at some other kind that forces her to think and to look for her own solutions. I am so accustomed to this kind of search that at times I prefer it to other types of work. Today, for example, while she was calling out the numbers and I was checking them on the adding-machine roll, I kept myself busy counting the little moles she has on her left arm. They divide themselves into two categories, five small marks and three large, of which one is really big. When she had finished calling out, "November," I said to her, just to see how she would react, "Have that beauty mark burned off. Generally nothing happens, but in one case in a hundred it could be dangerous." She turned all colors and didn't know where to put her arm. She said, "Thank you, sir," and kept on dictating to me, but was terribly uncomfortable. When we got to January, I began to call out and she made the checks. At one special moment I felt that something strange was happening, and I raised my eyes in the middle of a number. She was looking at my hand. In search of beauty marks? Perhaps. I smiled and once more she died of shame. Poor Avellaneda! She doesn't know that I am correct behavior in person, and that never, absolutely never, would I start anything with one of my employees.

THURSDAY, MARCH 21

I had dinner at the Vignales'. His house is stifling, dark, overstuffed. In the living room there are two armchairs in some indefinite international style, for all the world like a couple of armadillos. I let myself fall into one of them. As soon as I sat down I felt a hot sensation rising up to my chest. I had plumped on a little bleached-out bitch with the face of an old maid. She looked me over without sniffing me, then sprawled on the floor and committed the classic sin of lèse carpet. The stain remained there on the head of a royal peacock, which was the highpoint of that rather fearsome design. But there were so many such stains on the rug that in the end one could believe that they formed part of the decoration.

Vignale's family is numerous, noisy, oppressive. It includes his wife, mother-in-law, father-in-law, brother and sister-in-law, and—horror of horrors—his five children. These could be defined, with sufficient accuracy, as little monsters. In body they are normal—too normal, in fact—pink and healthy. Their monstrousness lies in the trouble they make. The oldest is thirteen (Vignale married quite late) and the youngest is six. They're constantly on the move, and constantly arguing at the top of their voices. You get the sensation that they're climbing on your back, on your shoulders, that they're always about to put their fingers in your ears or to pull your hair. They never get that far, but the effect is the same, and you're always aware that in Vignale's house you're at the mercy of a pack of hounds. The adults of the family have taken refuge in an enviable attitude of indifference; but that doesn't exclude some chance blows that suddenly fly through the air and land on the nose, ear or eye of one of those little angels. The method of their mother, for example, comes down to this: tolerate any posture or insolence of a child as long as it hurts someone else, including a visitor, but punish with violence every gesture or word of the urchin that hurts her personally. The culminating point of the meal took place at dessert. One of the children wanted to testify that he didn't care for the rice and milk. Said testimony consisting in throwing up his entire portion on his youngest brother's trousers. This act was celebrated with plenty of noise, but the racket raised by the damaged one surpassed all my expectations and defies description.

After dinner the kids disappeared, I don't know whether to bed or to prepare a poison cocktail for early tomorrow. "What children!" commented Vignale's mother-in-law. "They sure are alive." "That's what childhood is: life and nothing but," was the adequate summing-up by the son-in-law. Replying to a nonexistent question on my part, the sister-in-law informed me, "We don't have any children." "And we've been married seven years already," said her husband, with a loud and apparently malicious laugh. "For my part, I'd like to have some," explained his wife, "but he prefers to avoid them." It was Vignale who rescued all of us from what could have been a long discourse on gynecology and contraception, by bringing up the great attraction of the evening: the exhibition of the celebrated museum photos. He kept them in a green envelope, homemade out of wrapping paper, on which he had printed: "Photographs of Martin Santomé." It was evident that the envelope was old, but the legend pretty recent. On the first photo appeared four persons in front of the house in Brandzen Street. It wasn't necessary for Vignale to say a word: at sight of the photograph my memory shook itself and acknowledged the impact of that yellowish image that once had been in sepia. The ones in the doorway were my mother, a neighbor woman who later went off to Spain, my father and myself. My aspect was unbelievably unkempt and ridiculous. "That picture—did you take it yourself?" I asked Vignale. "Are you crazy? I never had the courage to handle a camera or a revolver. Falero took that snap. Do you remember Falero?" Vaguely. For example, that his father kept a bookshop, and that the son used to steal smutty magazines, taking care after reading them to spread among all of us that fundamental part of French culture. "Look at this other one," said Vignale eagerly. I was in that one too, next to the Doormat. This Doormat (I remember that nickname well) was an imbecile who always stuck close to us, laughed at all our jokes, even the least funny ones, and never left us, rain or shine. I didn't remember his real name, but I was sure that it was our "Doormat." The same boobyish expression, the same flabby flesh, the same plastered red hair. I burst out laughing—one of my best laughs of the year. "What are you laughing at?" asked Vignale. "At the Doormat. What a mess!" Then Vignale dropped his eyes, glanced shamefacedly at his wife and the others, and said in a hoarse voice, "I thought you had forgotten that nickname. I never liked being called by it." He took me entirely by surprise. I didn't know what to do, what to say. So Mario Vignale and the Doormat were one and the same? I looked at him, looked again, and saw once more that he was stupid, sticky, a real boob. But I saw a different kind of stupidity and boobery. The kind the Doormat had then he didn't have now. And now these traits had something incurable about them. I think I stammered, "But look, no one called you that with any malice. Remember that we all called Prado 'the Rabbit.'" "I wish they had called me 'the Rabbit,'" said Vignale, the Doormat, with regret in his voice. And we didn't look at any more photos.

I ran twenty yards to catch the bus, which was packed. When at last I got a seat I thought I was going to pass out. In the business of taking off my jacket, opening my shirt collar and moving a bit to get more air, I grazed once or twice the arm of a woman sitting next to me. It was a warmish arm, not too soft. In the contact I had the feeling of a velvety down, but I couldn't be sure whether it came from me, from her or from us both. I opened up my paper and started to read. She, in turn, was reading a tourist folder on Austria. In a short time I was breathing better, but the palpitations stayed with me for a full quarter of an hour. She moved her arm three or four times, but it didn't seem to want to separate itself completely from mine. It went away and came back. At times the contact was limited to a slight sensation of closeness at the very end of my hairs. I glanced toward the street several times, and in passing looked her over. An angular face, thin lips, long hair, little makeup, broad hands, not too expressive. All at once she dropped the brochure, and I bent down to pick it up. Naturally I shot a glance at her legs. Not bad, but with a Band-Aid on the ankle. She didn't thank me. As we passed Sierra Street, she began to get ready to leave. She held on to the brochure, straightened her hair, closed her pocketbook and asked my permission to pass. "I'm getting out too," I said, obeying an impulse. She began to walk quickly by way of Pablo de María Street, but in four strides I overtook her. We marched along, next to each other, for a block and a half. I was still formulating in my mind my opening words of attack, when she turned her head around toward me and said, "If you're going to speak to me, make up your mind."

SUNDAY, MARCH 24

Thinking it over, what a strange affair was that of Friday. We didn't tell our names, our phone numbers, or anything personal. However, I'd swear that sex isn't the chief interest of that woman. Rather she seemed exasperated by something, as if her giving herself to me was her curious form of vengeance against I don't know whom. I must confess that was the first time I conquered a woman just with my elbow; and also it was the first time, once we were in the furnished room, that a woman undressed herself before me so quickly in plain daylight. That aggressive shamelessness with which she lay down on the bed—what did that prove? She did so much to exhibit her complete nudity that I was ready to believe that it was actually the first time she found herself naked in front of a man. But she wasn't new at it. And with her serious face, her mouth without lipstick, her hands without expression, she still managed to get her full enjoyment. In the moment she deemed opportune, she asked me to say some dirty words. That isn't my specialty, but I think I left her satisfied.

MONDAY, MARCH 25

Esteban has a job with the city. It's the result of his work in the political club. I don't know if I should be glad about his being appointed a department head. He, coming from outside, moves above all the old-timers, who now will be his subordinates. My guess is that they'll make life impossible for him. And they'd be justified.

WEDNESDAY, MARCH 27

Today I stayed at the office until 11 P.M. An exploit of the general manager. He called me in at six-fifteen to tell me that he needed this piece of foolishness first thing tomorrow. It was a job for three persons. Avellaneda, poor thing, offered to stay. But I took pity on her.

Three fellows stayed on also in Deliveries. Actually their work was all that was really necessary. But evidently the director wasn't going to make Miss Valverde's lover work extra hours without inflicting the same punishment on some innocent fellow as well. This time I was that innocent. Patience. I just want the Valverde girl to get fed up with that gigolo of hers.

I become very depressed when I have to work overtime. The whole office silent, no customers, the desks messy, filled with file covers and all sorts of documents. The whole gives an impression of disorder and waste. And in the midst of that silence and darkness three guys here and three chaps there, working against their will, dragging along the fatigue of the eight previous hours.

Robledo and Santini called out the figures and I took them down on the machine. At 8 P.M. my back began to hurt, near the left shoulder. By nine I had become inured to the pain, and I just kept on writing the numbers they were hoarsely giving. When we finished no one spoke. The men in Deliveries had already left. We went off together to the Plaza, I treated them to coffee at the Sorocabana bar and we said good-bye. I think they were a little sore at me because I had picked them out to stay.

THURSDAY, MARCH 28

I had a long talk with Esteban. I explained my doubts about the fairness of his appointment. I didn't ask him to give it up; God knows and I know that sort of thing isn't in style. Simply, I would have liked to hear him say he felt uncomfortable. "There's nothing to worry about, old man. You're still living in another age." That's how he talked. "Now no one is offended if some guy or other comes from nowhere and passes him on the ladder. And do you know why no one gets mad? Because they'd all do the same thing if they had a chance. I'm sure that they're not going to look at me with resentment but rather with envy."

I told him . . . What's the difference what I told him?

FRIDAY, MARCH 29

What a disgusting wind. It was a triumph, and a tough one, for me to reach the Plaza along Ciudela Street starting from Colonia Street. The wind blew a girl's skirt over her head, and it blew the frock over the head of a priest. Jesus, what different sights! At times I wonder what would have happened if I had started out to be a priest. Probably nothing. I have a sentence I pronounce four or five times a year: "There are two professions for which I'm certain I haven't the slightest call: the military and the religious." But I believe I say that as an old habit, without the least conviction.

I reached the house worn out, with my throat burning

and my eyes full of dust. I washed, changed clothes and installed myself behind the window to take my maté. I felt protected. And also profoundly selfish. I saw passing men, women, oldsters, children, all struggling against the wind, and now with the rain as well. However, I felt no urge to open the door and call to them to take refuge in my house and keep me company with a hot maté. And it isn't that it didn't occur to me to do that. The idea came into my head, but I felt it was completely ridiculous, and I set to imagining the disconcerted expressions that the invited people would take on, even in the midst of the wind and the rain.

What would I have become, as of today, if twenty or thirty years ago I had decided to take priestly orders? Yes, I know what—the wind would blow up my frock and would leave exposed the trousers of a vulgar, undedicated man. But what of the rest? Would I have gained or lost? I wouldn't have children (I think I'd have been a sincere cleric, 100 percent chaste); I wouldn't have an office, or a work schedule. I wouldn't have my retirement. I'd have God, that indeed, and I'd have religion. But don't I have them anyway? Frankly, I don't know if I believe in God. At times I imagine that if God existed I wouldn't be so bothered with doubts. In reality, the faculties that he (or He?) himself has given us (reasoning power, sensibility, intuition) aren't in themselves sufficient to guarantee to us either his existence or his nonexistence. By a mere hunch I could believe in God and hit the mark, or not believe in God and hit the mark too. What then? Perhaps God has the face of a croupier, and I'm just a poor devil who plays red when black comes up, and vice versa.

Robledo is still sore at me, because of the additional work of last Wednesday. Poor guy. According to what Muñoz told me this morning, Robledo's fiancée is frightfully jealous of him. Last Wednesday he was due to meet her at 8 P.M., and because I chose him to stay late he couldn't make it. He notified her by telephone, but that wasn't good enough. The girl, already suspicious, told him she didn't want to have anything more to do with him. Muñoz says he consoled Robledo with the thought that it's always better to learn about these disadvantages before the marriage; but Robledo is in very bad humor. Today I called him over and explained to him that I hadn't known about his fiancée. I asked him why he hadn't mentioned it to me at the time, and then he looked at me with flashing eyes, and said in a low tone, "You did know about it. That farce of yours makes me sick." He sneezed, from pure nervousness, and added immediately, with a wide gesture of disappointment, "That the others, those good-for-nothings, should try to get me in trouble I can understand. But that you, a really serious man, should give me the same treatment, frankly that disillusions me a lot. I never said it to you, but I did have a good opinion of you." I was a little vexed that I had to defend his good opinion of my character, so I gave it to him straight: "Look, if you care to, you can believe me; and if not, just accept it. I didn't know anything. So let's end this matter, and you go back to work if you don't want me sore at you."

This afternoon, when I emerged from California Street, I saw at a distance the woman of the bus, her of the elbow. She was coming along with a stout chap who had an athletic look and about two fingers' worth of forehead. When the man laughed he made me think of the different ways that a man can look like an imbecile; she was laughing too, throwing her head back and leaning affectionately against him. They passed in front of me, and she saw me in the middle of a peal of laughter, but she didn't interrupt it. I couldn't be sure that she recognized me. Meanwhile she said to the big bruiser: "Oh, my darling one," and with a movement at once energetic and coquettish she brought her head against his necktie (it had giraffes on it). Then they turned into Ejido Street. Great question mark: What's the true connection between that gal and the one who the other afternoon undressed herself in record time?

Today they sent me instructions to take care of "the Jew who comes to ask for a job." Every two or three months he puts in an appearance here. The manager doesn't know how to get rid of him. He's a tall, splotched-faced fellow, about fifty years old, speaking a horrible Spanish, and perhaps writing it even worse. His set speech always contains the information that his specialties are correspondence in three or four languages, typing in German and cost accounting. He extracts from his wallet a letter, in a state of final deterioration, in which the chief of personnel in I don't know what institute in La Paz, Bolivia, certifies that Señor Franz Heinrich Wolff gave his services to their entire satisfaction, and left of his own will. However, the guy's expression is removed as far as possible from any hint of will, his own or anyone else's. By now we know from memory all his tics, his arguments, his air of resignation. For he invariably insists that we put him to the test; but when we set him before the typewriter the letter always comes out bad; to the few questions we put to him about it he replies with a tranquil silence. I can't imagine how he manages to live. His appearance is at once clean and wretched. He seems to be inexorably convinced of his bad luck; he doesn't grant himself the least possibility of success; but he does accept the obligation to continue stubbornly, without attaching much importance to all the refusals showered upon him. I wouldn't be able to say exactly whether the spectacle is pathetic, repugnant or sublime; but I believe that I'll never be able to forget the countenance (serene? resentful?) with which the man always receives the negative result of his test, and the semibow with which he departs. Sometimes I have seen him in the street, walking slowly or just gazing at the stream of people who pass and who perhaps inspire him to some reflection. I doubt if he'll ever be able to manage a smile. His look could be that of a crazy man, or of a wise man, or of one who makes believe, or of someone who has suffered much. But one thing is certain, and that is that every time I see him he leaves me with an uncomfortable feeling, and—worst of all—it is as if he knows that I am to blame. Of course, I know that's idiotic. I have no job in the office to offer him; what's more, he wouldn't do. And then? Perhaps I should know that there are other ways of helping a fellow man. But what ones? Advice, for example? I wouldn't want to think of the countenance with which he'd receive any of that. Today, after I told him no for the tenth time, I felt a little mouthful of pity come over me, and I decided to offer him my hand with a ten-peso note in it. He left me with my hand outstretched, looked at me fixedly (a pretty complicated look, though I think its principal ingredient was pity, in his turn), and said to me in that disagreeable accent, with its r's that sound like j's, "you don't compjehend." And that's entirely true. I don't understand; period. I don't want to think any more about all that.

TUESDAY, APRIL 2

I'm seldom with my children, especially Jaime. That's strange, because Jaime's precisely the one whom I'd like to see most often. Of the three he's the only one with a sense of humor. I don't know how much weight should be ascribed to "sympathy" in relations between father and child, but it's certain that, among the three, it's Jaime whom I find the most sympathetic. But, to offset it, he is also the least decipherable.

Today I saw him, but he didn't see me. A curious experience. I was at Convención and Colonia streets, saying good-bye to Muñoz, who had walked with me up to there. Jaime passed on the sidewalk in front of me. He was going with two others, who had something disagreeable in their gait or their costume; I don't remember that part well, because I paid special attention to Jaime. I didn't hear what he was saying to the others, but they were laughing overloudly. He kept serious, but his expression showed satisfaction; which might have come from the domination that at the moment he was exercising over his companions.

That evening I told him, "I saw you today at Colonia Street. You were walking with two others." It seemed to me that he turned red, but maybe I was wrong. "A companion at the office and his cousin," he said. "You seemed to be amusing them greatly," I added. "Oh, those two laugh at any nonsense."

Then, for the first time in his life, I believe, he asked me a question that referred to my own interests: "And . . . about when do you figure your retirement will be due?" Jaime asking about my retirement! I told him that Esteban had talked about it with a friend, to bring the matter to a head. But there's no way to expedite matters. It is necessary that, before anything is done, I get to be fifty. "And how do you feel about it?" he asked. "What do you think you'll do with so much time on your hands?" I laughed, and limited myself to a shrug. I said nothing, for two reasons. The first was that I still don't know what I'll do with my leisure. The second was that his sudden interest really moved me. A good day, this.

THURSDAY, APRIL 4

Once more we had to stay on late this afternoon. For a change the fault was ours; we had to look for a "difference." It was quite a problem to pick the people. Poor Robledo looked at me challengingly, but I didn't take him; I'd rather have him think that now he has the upper hand over me. Santini had a birthday party; Muñoz was going around with an ingrown toenail that kept him in very bad humor. Sierra had been absent for two days. At the end there remained Méndez and Avellaneda. At a quarter to eight Méndez approched me very mysteriously and asked me how much more time it was going to take. I told him at least until nine o'clock. Then, even more mysteriously and taking the greatest precautions so that Avellaneda wouldn't be listening, he confessed to me that he had a "heavy date" and that first he wanted to go home, to bathe, shave, change his clothes, etc. Still I made him suffer a little. I asked him, "Is she something choice?" "She's a poem, boss." They well know that the only weapon that conquers me is frankness. And they are more than frank. Obviously, I let him go.

Poor Avellaneda. Because we were left alone in the enormous place she became more nervous than usual. When she passed me a paper and I saw that her hand was trembling, I asked her point-blank, "Do I look that fierce? Don't be scared, Avellaneda." She laughed, and from that moment on she worked more calmly. It's quite a problem to talk to her. I always have to find a midpoint between the severe and the confidential. Three or four times I took a sly look at her. It's evident that she's a good girl. She has the definite marks of a loyal person. When her work bothers her somewhat, her hairdo gets disarranged, and that improves her looks. It wasn't until nine-ten that we found the difference. I asked her if she wanted me to accompany her home. "No, Señor Santomé, not at all." But while we walked toward the Plaza we talked about the work. She wouldn't accept a cup of coffee, either. I asked her where she lived, and with whom. Father and mother. A boyfriend? Outside of the office I must inspire less reverence, for she answered affirmatively and in a normal tone. "And when will we have to buy the present?" I asked, as is in order in such cases. "Oh, we've been going together for only a year." I believe that after having confessed to me that she had a boyfriend, she felt herself in a somewhat stronger position and she interpreted my questions as showing an almost paternal interest. She gathered all her courage to inquire if I was married, if I had children, etc. When I told her of my widowerhood she became very serious, and I think she was struggling between the ideas of a rapid change of subject and of taking part in my bereavement after twenty years had passed. Discretion won out, and she began to talk to me about her boyfriend. Scarcely had she informed me that he worked for the city when her trolley appeared. She shook hands with me and everything. What a pleasant surprise!

FRIDAY, APRIL 5

A letter from Aníbal. He's bored with São Paulo and is coming back at the end of the month. That's good news for me. I have only a few friends and Aníbal is the best. At least, he's the only one I can talk to about certain subjects without feeling ridiculous. Someday we'll have to investigate on what our friendship is based. He is Catholic, and I'm not anything. He's positive; I am routine and indecisive. It's certain that many times he pushes me into making a decision; other times it's I who restrain him by my doubts. When my mother died—it will be fifteen years in August—I was just annihilated. The only thing that held me up was a burning rage against God, my relatives and my neighbors. Every time I recall that interminable burial ceremony I become sick. The participants were divided into two classes: those who began to cry as they entered the door and then took me in their arms; and those who came only to put in an appearance, who gave me their hand with an irksome sympathy, and in ten minutes were telling dirty jokes. Then Aníbal arrived; he came up to me, but didn't even shake hands, and he began to talk very naturally: about me, about himself, about his family and also about my mother. This naturalness was a kind of balm, a true consolation; and I interpreted it as the best homage anyone could pay to my mother, and to myself in my grief for my mother. It was only a detail, an almost insignificant episode, that I realize; but it took place in one of those moments in which sorrow gives one an exaggerated receptivity.

SATURDAY, APRIL 6

A dream without head or tail. I had just crossed the Park of the Allies, dressed in pajamas. Suddenly, on the sidewalk before a luxurious two-story house, I saw that Avellaneda was there. I came to her without hesitation. She was wearing a simple garment, without ornaments or belt; somehow I knew she had nothing underneath it. She was seated on a kitchen bench, next to a eucalyptus, and she was peeling potatoes. All at once I noticed that it was nighttime, and I approached closer and said to her, "What a lovely smell of fields." It seems that my argument was decisive, for immediately I took possession of her, without encountering any resistance on her part.

This morning, when Avellaneda appeared in a simple costume, without ornaments or belt, I couldn't contain myself and I said to her, "What a lovely smell of fields." She looked at me with genuine panic, exactly as one looks at a crazy man or a drunk. Going from bad to worse, I tried to explain to her that I was talking to myself. I didn't convince her, and at noon, when she went off, she was still watching me with a certain mistrust. Another proof that it is possible to be more convincing in dreams than in reality.

Nearly every Sunday I take lunch and dinner alone, and inevitably I become melancholy. "What have I done with my life?" is a question that belongs to *Gardel* magazine, or the *Women's Supplement,* or to a *Reader's Digest* article. No matter. This Sunday I feel myself beyond the ridiculous, and I can ask myself questions of that type. In my personal history there were no irrational changes or unusual and sudden twists. The really special experience was the death of Isabel. Should I find in this death the true key to what I deem is my frustration? I don't think so. In truth, the more I investigate myself, the more I'm convinced that this early death was a catastrophe that, let us say, had good luck attached. (God, how that sounds vulgar and mean! I'm horrified at myself.) We were, then, in the full tide of desire. I believe that the most intense physical desire of my life was inspired by her. Would it be for that reason, maybe, that just as I'm unable to recon- struct (by my own imagination, and not with photographs or remembrance of remembrances) the face of Isabel, I can in exchange succeed in feeling in my hands, whenever I need to, the special touch of her waist, of her belly, of her legs, of her breasts. Why is it that my hands hold a more faithful memory than my memory itself? I can draw one consequence from that: if Isabel had lived enough years longer so that her body would have lost its bloom (it had this good thing: her skin was smooth and appealing in all its zones), and if, in the end, my capacity to desire her would also have faded, I couldn't guarantee what would have become of our exemplary marriage bond. For all of our harmony, which was surely there, depended unquestionably on the bed, our bed. I don't want that to imply that during the day we fought like cat and dog; on the contrary, in our daily life we always enjoyed a good measure of harmony. But what was it that restrained us from outbreaks or any overflow of ill temper? In all frankness, it was the enjoyments of the night, their protective presence in the midst of the menaces of the day. If sometimes we were tempted to quarrel and we began to compress our lips, there would pass before our eyes the spell of the nights, past or future, and then inevitably we would be engulfed in a wave of tenderness that banished all rancor. In saying that I'm not being inconsistent. My marriage was a good thing, a joyous season.

And what else is there? There is the opinion that one can hold of himself, something that (it's hard to believe) has very little to do with vanity. I refer to an opinion that is 100 percent sincere, an opinion that one wouldn't dare to confess even to the mirror before which one is shaving. I remember that there was a time (between my sixteenth and twentieth years) in which I held a good, almost an excellent opinion of myself. I felt the impulse to conceive and carry out "something great," to be useful to many people, to put things right. It shouldn't be said that my attitude was stupidly egocentric. Although I would have liked to enjoy the acceptance and even the applause of others, I believe that my first objective was not to use others but rather to be of use to them. I know that this isn't pure

Christian charity; however, the Christian idea of charity doesn't mean much to me. I remember that I had no purpose to help the needy, the crippled or the miserable (I have less and less faith in aid indiscriminately distributed). My intention was more modest; in all sincerity to be of use to my equals, to those who had a more legitimate right to need me.

In truth this excellent opinion about myself has fallen a lot. Today I seem to myself vulgar and, in some aspects, inexcusable. I could stand my way of living better if I didn't realize that in essence I am above such vulgarity. In the intellectual sense, of course. To know that I have, or at least had, in myself sufficient qualities to make more of myself; to know that I am superior, if not too much so, to the rhythm I have given my life—to know all that doesn't make me any more serene, rather it makes me feel more frustrated and less apt to value myself above my circumstances. Worst of all is that no frightful events brought me low (true, Isabel's death was a powerful blow, but I couldn't call it frightful; is there anything more natural than for someone to depart from this world?), nothing occurred which restrained my best impulses, impeded my development and chained me to lethargic routine. I myself have created my routine, and with the simplest of purposes: accumulation. The very fact that I knew myself capable of something better placed in my hands the weapon of procrastination, which, to sum it up, is a terrible and suicidal arm. From that it eventuated that my routine never seemed definitive; I've always considered it provisional, a temporary course, to be followed only as long as the procrastination lasted. Its role was to help me support my daily duties during that period of preparation which apparently I considered unavoidable, before I embarked on the realization of what my destiny owed to me. Wasn't that stupid vanity? One result of all that is that now I have no important vices (I smoke little; and only from boredom do I take a drink now and then). But I believe that now I shouldn't be able to stop my procrastination; that is my true vice, and what's more, it's incurable. For if now I should announce to myself, in a long-delayed formal declaration, "I am going to be exactly what I always wanted to be," it would all turn out to be useless. First, because my powers are too limited to subject them to a change of my mode of life; and second, because the man I wanted to be has no validity for me now. It would be somewhat as if I were to launch myself consciously into a premature old age. What I want now is much more modest than what I wanted thirty years ago, and—above all—it is much less important for me to obtain it. To retire, for example. It's an aspiration of a sort, but it's an aspiration downward. I know my retirement will arrive, I know it's coming by itself, I know that it won't require achievement on my part. In that way, it's easy. A decision that can be made like that is worth the little trouble it takes.

TUESDAY, APRIL 9

This morning Doormat Vignale called up. I had him told that I wasn't in, but when he called me again in the afternoon I felt obliged to talk to him. That's a principle with me. If I have a good sort of relationship with people (I wouldn't dare to call it friendship) it's perhaps because I deserve it.

He wants to come to my house. "Something confidential,

old man. I can't tell you over the phone, and I couldn't ask you here for that." We agreed on Thursday night. He'll come after dinner.

WEDNESDAY, APRIL 10

Avellaneda has something that attracts me. That's evident, but what is it?

THURSDAY, APRIL 11

It's a half hour before dinnertime. Vignale is coming tonight. Only Blanca and I will be here. The boys disappeared as soon as they heard about the visit. I don't blame them. In their place I too would have escaped.

There's been a change in Blanca. She has color in her cheeks, and it isn't artificial; she has color even after washing her face. At times she forgets that I'm in the house and begins to sing. She hasn't much of a voice, but she handles it with good taste. It pleases me to hear her. What is going on in my children's heads? Could they be in a period of aspiration *upward?*

FRIDAY, APRIL 12

Yesterday Vignale arrived at 11 P.M. and left at two in the morning. His problem fits into a few words: his sister-in-law is in love with him. I think it's worthwhile to transcribe, even only approximately, the version given by Vignale. "Keep in mind that they have been living with us for the past six years. Six years are not a few days. I don't mean to say that up to now nothing had drawn my attention to Elvira. You must have noticed that she's pretty enough. And if you saw her in a bathing suit you'd be knocked off your feet. But, gosh! It's one thing to look and another to profit. What is there to say? My boss lady has a bit too much flesh, and besides, she's constantly put out of humor by the work of the house and the care of the kids. You can imagine that after fifteen years of marriage it's not a matter of just seeing her and ipso facto being inflamed with passion. Furthermore, she has menstrual periods that last about two weeks; so it's pretty difficult for my desires to coincide with her availability. The truth is that many times I go about sex-hungry and I dine with my eyes on the legs of Elvira—who, to make matters worse, always wears shorts in the house. The trouble is that the woman has given my glances the wrong meaning; rather, she interpreted them right, but a bit too far. The real truth is that if I had known that Elvira liked me, I wouldn't have looked at her that way, for the last thing I want is to cause a fuss in my own home, which for me has always been sacred. First there was her looking at me and me acting stupid. But the other day she crossed her legs, only that, in shorts, and I couldn't keep myself from saying, 'Be careful.' She answered, 'I don't want to be careful,' and that started a dispute. As it went on she asked me if I was blind; I knew very well that she wasn't indifferent toward me, etc., etc. Though I was sure that it wouldn't help matters, I recalled to her that she has a husband, who is my brother-in-law— and do you know what she replied? 'Who? That no-account?' And the worst of it is that she's right. Francisco is a cipher. That has reduced my scruples somewhat. What would you do in my place?"

If I were in his place I wouldn't have his problems. First,

because I wouldn't have married his idiot of a wife; and second, I wouldn't have been attracted in any way by the white skin of the other middle-aged siren. But I couldn't tell him anything but commonplaces. "Be careful. Watch out that you don't fall into her clutches, with no available exit. If you want to get into a jam with your whole family situation, then go ahead; but if, as you say, that situation is more important to you than anything else, then don't risk it." He left, feeling remorseful, troubled, undecided. I believe, however, that Francisco's marital front is in danger.

SUNDAY, APRIL 14

This morning I took a bus and got out at Agraciada and Nineteenth of April streets. It's years since I was there last. I had the illusion that I was visiting an unknown city. Only now I realized that I have become accustomed to living in streets that have no trees. And how irremediably cold such streets can be.

One of the most agreeable things in life is to see the sun filtering through the leaves.

It was a good morning today. But in the afternoon I took a siesta of four hours and I got up in a bad humor.

TUESDAY, APRIL 16

I still don't know what attracts me in Avellaneda. Today I was studying her. She moves well, she pats back her hair gracefully, and on her cheeks she has a light fuzz, like the down of a peach. What would she be doing with her boyfriend? Do they act like a decent couple, or do they get hot like any youngsters of the neighborhood? That's a key question for me. Is it envy?

WEDNESDAY, APRIL 17

Esteban said that if I want to have my retirement by the end of the year I would have to begin now. He says he's going to help me to get it going, but even then it will take time. "To help get it going" means greasing somebody's palm. I wouldn't like that. I know that the other fellow would be most to blame, but I wouldn't be innocent, either. Esteban's theory is that we must solve our problems in the manner required by our surroundings. What in one environment would be simply honest, in another would be simply imbecile. He's partly right, but it bothers me that he's right.

THURSDAY, APRIL 18

The inspector came; amiable, with whiskers. No one would have thought that he was going to be such a nuisance. He began by asking for the figures of our last trial balance and he finished by wanting a separate list of the subdivisions figuring in the opening inventory. I spent the day trotting out old and tattered books from early morning to the last hour of the afternoon. The inspector was very nice. He smiled, begged pardon and said, "Thanks a lot." An enchanting fellow—why doesn't he drop dead? At the beginning I stored up my rage, answering between my teeth, cursing him mentally. Afterward that strong language gave way to another feeling. I began to feel old. Those dates that begin in 1929—it was I who wrote them; those entries and counterentries that figured in the first drafts of the journal—it was I who had written them; those figures brought forward in pencil in the cash book—I wrote them too. In those days I was only a beginner, but they were already giving me important things to do, although the little glory therefore went to the chief, just as now I gain a bit of glory from the important things done by Muñoz and Robledo. I feel myself a little like the Herodotus of the enterprise, the registrar and scribe of its history, the one surviving witness. Twenty-five years. Five *lustra*. Or a quarter century. No. It's much more impressive to say, simply and plainly, twenty-five years. And how my penmanship has changed! In 1929 I had an uneven handwriting: the small *t*'s didn't lean the same way as the *d*'s, *b*'s or *h*'s—as if they had not been blown upon by the same wind. In '39, the lower halves of the *f*'s, *g*'s and *j*'s have somewhat the appearance of indecisive flecks, without character or will. In 1945 I began the era of capital letters; I liked adorning them with large curves, spectacular and useless. The *M* and the *H* were great spiders, with their web and all. But not now. Now my handwriting has become synthetic, regular, disciplined, clean. The only thing that proves this change a make-believe is that I myself have turned complicated, irregular, chaotic, unclean. All at once, when the inspector asked me for a date back in 1930, I recognized my improved handwriting as that of a special time. With the same penmanship that I wrote, "Details of salaries paid to the personnel for the month of August, 1930"—yes, in the same lettering and the same year I had written twice a week, "Beloved Isabel." For Isabel was living then in Melo, and I wrote to her punctually on Tuesdays and Fridays. So that had been the handwriting of my engagement period. I smiled, and the inspector smiled with me. Then he asked me for another set of accounts.

[46]

SATURDAY, APRIL 20

Shall I be all dried up? Sentimentally, I mean.

MONDAY, APRIL 22

New confession of Santini. Referring again to his little seventeen-year-old sister. He says that when their parents are not home she comes into his room, and dances almost naked before him. "She has one of those two-piece bathing suits; you know that kind? Well, when she comes to dance in my room she takes off the upper piece." "And you, what do you do?" "Me—I get nervous." I told him if he only got nervous, there was no danger. "But, sir, that's immoral!" he said, waving his wrist with the little chain and the medal. "And she—what reasons does she give for dancing in front of you with so little clothes on?" "Imagine this, sir. She says that I don't care for women, and she's going to cure me of that." "And is that right?" "Well, even if it is right, she shouldn't be doing what she does—for her own sake, it seems to me." Then I resigned myself to asking the question that he had been going after for some time. "And men—do you like *them*?" Again he jangled the little chain and the medal. He said, "But that's immoral, sir." And he gave me a wink halfway between the cute and the disgusting. "Don't you think so too?" I told him to go chase himself, and gave him the rottenest job I could think of. Now he won't be able to raise his head for at least ten days. That's all I needed—a fairy in my department. It seems he's of the type "with scruples." What a jewel! One thing is certain, nevertheless—that little sister is quite a number.

WEDNESDAY, APRIL 24

Today, as always on April 24, we had dinner together. Good reason. Esteban's birthday. I think we all felt somewhat obliged to be jovial. Even Esteban appeared quite normal; he cracked some jokes, and received our embraces without flinching.

The menu prepared by Blanca was the high point of the evening. Naturally that also was an influence toward good humor. It's not at all absurd that a chicken à la Portuguese leaves me more optimistic than a potato omelet. Hasn't it occurred to any sociologist to make a modest study of the effect of our eating habits upon the culture, the economy and the politics of Uruguay? My God, how we eat! In joy, in grief, in amazement, in collapse. Our sensibility is primordially digestive. Our innate devotion to democracy rests upon an old postulate: "We all have to eat." Our religious people are only mildly interested in whether God forgives their transgressions, but to make up for that they pray on bended knees, with tears in their eyes, that they won't lack for their daily bread. And that daily bread is not—I'm sure of it—a mere symbol; it's a German loaf weighing a full two pounds.

OK. We ate well, had a good claret, drank a toast to Esteban. At the end of the dinner, as we slowly stirred our coffee, Blanca dropped a piece of news. She has a boyfriend. Jaime wrapped her in an unusual and indefinite glance. (What is Jaime? Who is Jaime? What does Jaime want?) Esteban asked cheerfully the name of the "unlucky guy." I think I felt happy and I let it show through. "When shall we get to know this choice morsel?" I asked. "Look, Dad, Diego won't make formal visits on Mondays, Wednesdays and Fridays. We meet at various places—downtown, in his house, here." When she said "in his house," we must all have frowned, for she hastened to add, "He lives with his mother, in an apartment. Don't be afraid." "And his mother—doesn't she ever go out?" asked Esteban, a bit sarcastic. "Don't get funny," Blanca said, and right away she asked me, "Papá, I'd like to know if you have confidence in me. That's the only judgment I'm interested in. Do you trust me?" When they put that kind of question to me point-blank, there's only one thing I can reply. My daughter knows that. "Of course I trust you," I said. Esteban limited himself to showing he was still incredulous by noisily clearing his throat. Jaime continued silent.

FRIDAY, APRIL 26

The general manager called another meeting of department heads. Suárez wasn't there; he happened to have the grippe. Martínez took advantage of the occasion to speak out some truths. He did very well. I admire his energy. As for me, at bottom I don't give a hang for the office, titles, the pecking order and other things of show. I was never attracted by the hierarchy. My secret motto has been, "The lower the title, the less the responsibility." The truth is that one lives more comfortably without heavy duties. But Martínez is doing the right thing for himself. Among all the heads, the only ones who could aspire to being assistant manager (a place to be filled at the end of the year) would be, in order of seniority, myself, Martínez and Suárez.

Martínez has nothing to fear from me, for he knows that I'm taking my retirement. On the other hand, he is afraid of Suárez (and with reason) for he knows that since the latter has taken up with Valverde's daughter he has made notable progress; from assistant cashier he passed to first grade official in the middle of last year, and from that to head of the shipping department only about four months ago. Martínez knows perfectly well that the only way of defending himself against Suárez is to discredit him completely. Certainly for that he doesn't have to imagine things too much, given that Suárez, in terms of accomplishment, is a calamity. The fellow knows he has immunity; he knows he is hated, but scruples have never been his specialty.

You should have seen the manager's face when Martínez shot the works. Martínez asked him directly if "you, Mr. Manager, happen to know if any other member of the board of directors has a daughter available for sleeping with heads of departments," adding that he was subject to call. The boss asked him what he was after; did he want to be suspended? "Not at all," explained Martínez. "I'm looking for a promotion. I understood that's the way to get ahead." The manager merely said, "Too bad." The chief knows that Martínez is right, but he knows also that there is nothing he can do about it. For the present, at least, Suárez can't be touched.

SUNDAY, APRIL 28

Aníbal has arrived. I went to meet him at the airport. He's softer, older, more worn out. Nevertheless, it was a joy to see him again. We didn't talk much, because his three sisters were there, and I never got along well with those flighty girls. We left it that we'd see each other soon; he'll call me at the office.

MONDAY, APRIL 29

Today my section was a desert. Three of the crew showed up missing. Furthermore, Muñoz was out somewhere and Robledo had to go over the slips with the Sales Department. It's not so bad, because at this time of the month there isn't much work. The rush always comes after the first. I took advantage of the solitude and the scarcity of work to chat awhile with Avellaneda. For some days now I've noticed she was rather lifeless, depressed. Yes, I could feel her sadness. It sharpened her features, gave her eyes a melancholy look, but somehow made her look younger. I like Avellaneda. I think I wrote that once. I asked her what was going on with her. She came up to my desk, smiled at me (how nicely she smiles), but said nothing. "For some days now I've noticed you are without spirit, as if you were grieving," I said, after which, to give my remarks the same stock of words as my thought, I added, "That's right, I can feel that you're sad." She didn't take it as a play of gallantry. She only lit up her melancholy eyes and said, "You're very kind, Señor Santomé." God in heaven! The first part of her answer had sounded so nice. But then the "Señor Santomé" recalled to me my nearly fifty years; the words put a pitiless end to my vain yearnings, and left me only the strength to ask her in a tone falsely paternal, "The boyfriend?" Poor Avellaneda eye's filled with tears, she shook her head in a gesture that seemed an affirmation, stammered an "Excuse me," and exited running to the ladies' room. I remained for a while not knowing what to do, with my papers before me; I think I was really moved. I felt agitated, as I hadn't felt for a long time. And it wasn't the usual nervousness of a man who sees a woman crying or on the verge. My agitation was my own, only for myself; the agitation of witnessing my own emotion. Suddenly a light dawned in my mind. So I am not dried up! When Avellaneda returned, now minus her tears and a little ashamed, I was still selfishly enjoying my new discovery. I'm not dried up, I'm not dried up! Then I looked at her with gratitude; and as Muñoz and Robledo came in at that moment, we both went back to work as if by a secret agreement.

TUESDAY, APRIL 30

We'll have to see what's happening to me. The whole day there passed through my head, like a recurrent refrain, the single sentence "So she's had a fight with her boyfriend." And my rate of breathing went up and up. The same day I discovered that I hadn't dried out, I felt a strange mixture of excitement and egoism. Well, in spite of all, I think that marks a step ahead.

WEDNESDAY, MAY 1

The most boring Workers' Day of all history. To make things worse, it was gray, rainy, like a premature winter. The streets without people, without buses, with nothing. And I in my room, in my big bed for one person, in that dark, heavy silence of six-thirty in the morning. If only it were already 9 A.M. and I were at my desk, and from time to time I could look toward the left and would find that little face—sad, concentrating, defenseless.

THURSDAY, MAY 2

No, I don't want to have a talk with Avellaneda. First, because I don't want to scare her; second, because I don't really know what to say to her. Before a talk I'd have to know precisely what is happening to me. It can't be true that at my age there suddenly appears this girl, who isn't even definitely pretty, and becomes the center of my attention. I feel as nervous as an adolescent, that's sure; but when I look at my skin that is beginning to get flabby, when I see those wrinkles around my eyes, those varicose veins in my ankles, when I hear in the mornings my old man's cough (which is necessary to let my bronchial tubes begin their day), then I don't feel adolescent, but ridiculous.

The whole mechanism of my feelings stopped twenty years ago, after Isabel died. First I felt grief, then indifference, later a sense of liberty, finally boredom. A long, solitary, unchanging boredom. Oh, yes; during all these stages sex continued active. But the technique was strictly "à la carte." Today a "pickup" found in the bus, tomorrow a government employee who checks our accounts; the day after, the cashier of the Lamas department store. Never twice with the same one. A kind of unconscious resistance against compromising myself, against encasing my future in a normal relationship on a permanent basis. Why all those precautions? What was being defended? The image of Isabel? I don't think so. I didn't feel that I had to sacrifice myself to this sort of sentimental contract, which in any case I never signed. My liberty? That could be. My liberty is another name for my inertia. To go to bed today with one woman, tomorrow with another (well, that's just an expression, it has now become once a week). What human nature demands and nothing more—like eating, bathing, going to the toilet. With Isabel it was different because we had a sort of communion and when we made love it seemed that every hard bone of mine corresponded with a soft bone of hers, that every impulse of mine found itself coordinated with its echo. This against that. It's just like when one becomes accustomed to dancing with the same partner. At first every movement induces a corresponding response; then the response corresponds immediately to every thought. There is only one person who thinks, but the two bodies make the dance step.

SATURDAY, MAY 4

Aníbal has phoned me. We'll see each other tomorrow. Avellaneda didn't show up at the office. Jaime asked me for money. He had never done that before. I asked him what he needed it for. "I can't and I won't tell you. If you want to, lend it to me, and if not, keep it. It's all the same to me." "The same?" "Yes, the same. For if I have to pay this humiliating price of opening up to you my intimate life, my heart, my guts, etc., I prefer to look for the money somewhere else, where they only ask me to pay interest." I gave him the money, of course. But why all that violence? A mere question isn't an exorbitant price. The worst of it all, and what gets me most angry, is that generally I ask questions like that merely from absent-mindedness; actually the last thing I want is to push myself into the private zones of other people, especially of my children. But Jaime, equally with Esteban, is always in a state of near-conflict in whatever concerns me. Now we have tremendous quarrels; well, then, let them adjust themselves as they can.

SUNDAY, MAY 5

Aníbal is not the same man. I always had the secret impression that he was going to be eternally young. But it seems that eternity has come, and it has not found him young. He has deteriorated physically. He's grown thin, his bones show more, his clothes seem too large, his mustache is now skimpy. But it isn't only that. From the tone of his voice, which seems thicker to me than I remember it, to the movements of his hands, which have lost their vivacity; from his expression, which in the first moment appeared feeble, but which afterward gave me to understand that he is only disenchanted, to his subjects of conversation, which used to be full of jokes and are now unbelievably gray—all combine into a single affirmation: Aníbal has lost his joie de vivre.

He said scarcely anything about himself; I mean, he spoke only superficially about himself. He has gotten together some money, it seems. He wants to set up a business here, but he still hasn't decided in what field. But at least this is true: he is still interested in politics.

That's not my forte. I realized that fact when he began to ask me questions, more and more incisive, as if he were seeking explanations for things he hadn't been able to understand. He made me realize that I didn't have well-formed opinions about those topics that from time to time one bats about in gossip at the office or the café, or about which we have vague side thoughts while we read the newspaper at breakfast. Aníbal forced me to recognize this failure, and I think that my thoughts crystallized somewhat as I answered him. He asked me if I believed that all was better or worse than five years ago, when he left. "Worse," answered every cell in my body, as one. But then I had to explain. Phew, what a task!

For, in truth, bribery has always existed here, compromises too, wheeling and dealing the same. So what is worse now? After lots of cerebration my brain reached the conviction that what is worse now is our acceptance of it all. The rebels have turned into semirebels, the semirebels into resigned people. I believe that in our shining Montevideo the two groups that have made the most progress in these times are the pederasts and those who have given up. "We can't do anything about it," people say. Previously people gave bribes when they wanted to do something illegal. That's understandable. But now we also hand out bribes to be allowed to do something legal. And that means that all standards are gone.

But there's more to it than mere acceptance. At the beginning there was resignation; afterward, the loss of scruples; finally, participation. It was an ex-resigned one who pronounced the celebrated phrase "If the higher-ups swallow it, I'll swallow it too." Naturally, the ex-resigned one has an excuse for his dishonesty. It's the only way that all the others can't take advantage of him. He can say that he was forced to get into the game; for as it was, his wealth was constantly diminishing and hence more and more straight paths were closing to him. But at least he continues to hold a vengeful hatred against those pioneers who forced him to follow their route. Perhaps, after all, the most hypocritical of the lot might be the man who now does nothing to get ahead. Perhaps he is also the most dishonest, because he knows perfectly well that no one dies of honesty.

It really was peculiar, my not being accustomed to think about all that Aníbal said. He left as dawn came, and I found myself so disturbed that I couldn't think of Avellaneda.

TUESDAY, MAY 7

There are two procedures for approaching Avellaneda: (a) frankness—to say to her in a few words, "I like you, let's see what happens"; (b) showing off—telling her something like this: "Look, girl, I'm experienced. I could be your father. Listen to my advice." Although it seems incredible, perhaps the second is better suited for me. With the first approach I risk a lot, and besides, everything is still too undeveloped. I believe that up to now she has seen in me a more or less amiable boss and nothing more. However, she isn't such a kid. Twenty-four years aren't fourteen. She's one of those who prefer mature types. But her boyfriend was a youngster, who didn't amount to much. OK, that's how it was with him. So much the better; now, as a reaction, she'll go to the other extreme. And at that other extreme could be me, a mature gentleman, experienced, white-haired, quiet, forty-nine years, without major vices, drawing a good salary. As to my three children, I don't count them in the picture; they're no help. In any case, she knows I have them.

Well, now—to say it in terms of the neighborhood gossips —what are my intentions? The truth is that I haven't decided to think about anything permanent, like "till death do us part." (I wrote "death" and right away Isabel appeared. But Isabel was someone else; I think that in Avellaneda I'm concerned less with the sexual side—that might well be because sex is less important at forty-nine years of age than at twenty-eight). But I'm not willing to give up on Avellaneda, either. The ideal, I know, would be to have Avellaneda without any permanent obligation. But that's asking a lot. Still, I could try it.

Until I talk to her, I can't know anything. These are only stories that I'm making up. It's certain that, at this stage, I'm a little tired of chance assignations, of meetings in furnished rooms. There's always a hollow atmosphere and a sensation of "right away," of something urgent, in any kind of dialogue that I carry on with any sort of woman. Up to the moment of going to bed with her, whoever she may be, the important thing is to go to bed with her; after making love the important thing is to get away, each returning to his own place, and to lose contact forever after. In years and years of that game I don't recall a single comforting conversation, not even a single moving phrase (mine or the other's), of the kind that are destined to reappear afterward, who knows in what confused moment, to end some vacillation, to help us to take an attitude that demands at least a minimum dose of courage. Well, that isn't entirely correct. In a furnished room on Rivera Street, it must be six or seven years ago, a woman said this sentence to me: "You make love like a man doing a job," and at least I've always remembered that.

THURSDAY, MAY 9

I can't speak to her in the office. It will have to be somewhere else. I am studying her itinerary. She eats at times at the Center. She lunches with a friend, a stout girl employed at "London, Paris." But then they separate, and she stops for a demitasse at a café at Twenty-fifth and Missions. It will have to be a casual meeting.

FRIDAY, MAY 10

I've met Diego, my future son-in-law. First impression, I like him. He has decision in his look, he speaks with a kind of pride, which (it seems to me) is not without reason—i.e., it is based on something solid in his character. He treats me with respect, without fawning on me. In his whole attitude there's something that pleases me, and I believe it pleased my vanity too. He was predisposed in my favor, that's evident; and what other source could that good attitude have if not from his conversations with Blanca? I should be truly happy, in that area at least, knowing that my daughter has a good opinion of me. It's strange; I don't care, for example, what opinion I deserve from Esteban. But I do care, and quite a lot, that's sure, what opinion I deserve from Jaime and from Blanca. Perhaps the reason, and I've searched it out, consists in this: despite the fact that all three mean a lot to me, despite the fact that in all three I see reflected many of my own impulses and inhibitions, in Esteban I note besides a species of hidden enmity, a variant of hate, which he doesn't even dare to confess to himself. I don't know which came first, his drawing back or my own, but it's certain that I, on my part, don't love him the way I love the others, that I feel myself distant from that son who doesn't ever stay at home, who addresses words to me as if by obligation, and who gives all the symptoms of being "a stranger in his family." Jaime doesn't seem much inclined to communicate with me either, but I don't see in him that type of involuntary drawing away. At bottom, Jaime suffers from a solitude that has no cure, and all those around him must bear the consequences.

Getting back to Diego, I'm happy the boy has character; that will be good for Blanca. He's a year younger than she, but looks four or five years older. The essential thing is that she should feel protected; in return, Blanca is loyal, she won't cheat him. I'm pleased that they go out together and alone, without a cousin or a little sister accompanying them. Comradeship is a nice stage; it has no substitute and it can't be recovered. That's something for which I can never excuse Isabel's mother; during our engagement she stuck to us like a porous plaster; she watched us so closely and so jealously that, even if I had been the acme of purity, I would have felt obliged to invoke all the sinful thoughts at my disposal. To the point that on those occasions—very rare, that's certain—when she wasn't present we didn't feel alone; we were sure that a kind of phantom with a scarf was registering all our movements. If sometimes we kissed each other we were under such a strain, so intent on detecting the least warning of her appearance in any one of the four cardinal points of the living room, that the kiss turned out to be no more than a momentary contact, with very little sex and even less tenderness. But on the other hand it brought us a lot of apprehension, it created a kind of short circuit that damaged our nerves. That woman is still alive; the other afternoon I saw her on Sarandi Street, tall as corn, resolute, indestructible, accompanying the youngest of her six daughters and with an ugly chap who had the appearance of a fiancé in custody. The girl and her suitor didn't walk arm in arm; there was a space between them at least eight inches wide. I saw that the old woman still hadn't given up her famous declaration: "The arm when you're married."

But I'm again getting away from the subject of Diego. He says he's working in an office, but it's only provisional. "I can't accept the prospect of seeing myself always there, locked in, swallowing the odor of antiquity from my books. I'm sure I'm going to be and do other things; I don't know if better or worse than what I'm doing now, but different." I too had a period in which I thought like that. But . . . but . . . That chap appears more decided than I was.

SATURDAY, MAY 11

One time I heard her say that Saturdays at noon she meets a cousin of hers at Eighteenth and Paraguay. I *must* talk to her. Today I spent an hour at that corner, but she didn't come. I can't make a date with her; it must be casual.

SUNDAY, MAY 12

I've also heard her say that on Sundays she goes to the amusement park. I had to talk with her, so I went to the place. Two or three times it seemed to me that she was there. In the crowd I suddenly saw among all those heads a part of a neck or a hairdo or a shoulder that seemed to be hers, but later the figure completed itself and the part I had observed joined itself to the rest and lost its resemblance to her. Sometimes a woman viewed from the back had her walk, her hips, her nape. But all at once she turned around and the likeness changed into an absurdity. The only thing that doesn't fool you (as a single trait) is the facial expression. Nowhere did I find her eyes. However (only now the thought comes to me), I don't know what they are like, of what color. I got home tired, dizzy, annoyed, bored. But there's another word, more exact. I came home alone.

MONDAY, MAY 13

They are green. Gray-green. I was looking at her, perhaps too attentively, and then she asked me, "What's wrong with me, sir?" How ridiculous that she calls me "sir." "Your face is smudged," I said, like a coward. She passed her index finger over her cheek (a quite characteristic gesture of hers, which draws her eye downward and doesn't suit her), and asked again, "And now?" "Now it's OK," I answered with a little less cowardice. She smiled, and I was able to add, "Now you're not OK; now you're pretty." I think she was impressed by that. I think that now she knows something is going on. Or could she have interpreted it as parental affection? It disgusts me to feel parental.

WEDNESDAY, MAY 15

I was in the café at Twenty-fifth and Missions. From 12:30 to 2 P.M. I was trying an experiment. "I have to speak to her," I thought. "Consequently she'll have to appear." I began to "see her" in every woman who approached Twenty-fifth Street. This time I didn't care very much if I couldn't recognize a single detail in each figure to remind me of her. Just the same I "saw" her. A kind of magic game (magic or idiotic, it all depends on the angle one looks from). Only when the woman came within a few steps of me would I beat a mental retreat and stop looking at her, substituting the imagined form for the unwanted reality. Until, suddenly, the miracle came. A girl appeared at the corner, and right away I saw in her Avellaneda, the image of Avellaneda. But when I wanted to make my now accustomed retreat it happened that the reality also was Avellaneda. How my heart jumped! I thought it had come up to my throat. She was two steps away, next to my window. I said, "Hello. What are you up to?" The tone was natural, at most routine. She looked surprised. I believe agreeably surprised—if only it could be agreeably surprised! "Oh, Señor Santomé, you gave me a fright." A single, almost indifferent gesture of my right hand, to accompany an invitation devoid of emphasis. "A cup of coffee?" "No, I can't, too bad. My father is waiting for me at the bank; we've something to do there." That's the second time she said no to my cup of coffee, but all I answered now was, "Too bad!" If I hadn't said that I think I would have thrown a glass on the floor, or bit my lower lip, or dug my nails into my fingertips. No; it's silly to write that. I wouldn't have done anything of the kind. But I did have a brief paroxysm that left me out of breath and empty, with my leg bent, my teeth clenched and my eyes hurting from looking so long at the same coffee spoon. But I was able to say, "Too bad"; and then before she left, she asked, "Are you always here at this time?" "Yes indeed," I lied. "Then let's put off your invitation for another day." "Fine; now don't forget it," I insisted, and away she went. When, five minutes later, the waiter came and brought me more coffee, he said, looking toward the street, "What a pretty little package, eh? It makes you feel like new. You want to sing and everything." Only then could I hear myself. Unconsciously, like an old gramophone on which one puts a record and then forgets it, I had started—quite unconsciously—on the second stanza of "My Flag."

THURSDAY, MAY 16

"You'll never guess who I met," said the voice of Vignale over the phone. My silence was undoubtedly so provoking that he couldn't wait even three seconds before blurting out the answer. "Escayola; imagine that." I imagined. Escayola? A rare thing to hear that name again, an echo from the old days, one of those that don't turn up now. "You don't say. And how is he?" "He's a barrel; he weighs two hundred and fifteen pounds." Of course Vignale has told Escayola about meeting me, and—naturally—a dinner figures in the program.

Escayola. He too is of the period of Brandzen Street. But I remembered him right away. He was a light, tall and nervous youth; for everything he had a joking comment and his chatter was generally amusing. In the café of Álvarez the Galician, Escayola was the star. Evidently we were all predisposed to laughter; for that boy could say anything (it didn't have to be very witty) and right away we were in stitches. I remember that we screamed with laughter, holding our sides. I think the secret was that he made himself the funny man with a deadpan look: a kind of Buster Keaton. It would be nice to see him again.

FRIDAY, MAY 17

At last it happened. I was in the café, sitting near the window. That time I wasn't expecting anything, I wasn't watching out. I think I was making calculations, in a vain effort to balance the expenses against the income of this May so tranquil, truly autumnal, and chock-full of debts. I raised my eyes, and there she was. Like an apparition, or a phantom, or simply—and how much better—like Avellaneda. "I've come to claim the coffee of the day before yesterday," she said. I stood up, I banged against my chair, and my coffee spoon fell from the table with a racket that seemed rather to come from a tablespoon. The waiters looked on. She sat down. I picked up the coffee spoon, but before I could get seated my jacket caught in those damn nails that all the café seats have along their sides. (In my general program for this so longed-for interview I hadn't taken into account a mise-en-scène as exciting as that. "It looks as if I scared you," she said, laughing in an open way. "Well, yes, a little," I confessed, and that saved me. Everything became natural. We spoke of the office, of some of our co-workers, I recounted some anecdotes of times past. She laughed at them. She wore a little jacket of dark green over a white blouse. Her hairdo was awry, but only the right half, as if a gust of wind had reached her on that side. I told her so. She took a little mirror out of her purse, looked at herself and was amused for a while by the ridiculous sight. I was pleased that her good humor carried her so far as to make fun of herself. Then I said, "Do you know that you are responsible for one of the most important crises in my life?" She asked, "Economic?" and laughed again. I replied, "No, sentimental," and I became serious. "Gosh," she said, and waited for me to continue. And I went on. "Look, Avellaneda, it's very possible that what I'm going to say will seem crazy to you. If that's the way it is, just say so. But I don't want to beat about the bush. I think I'm in love with you." I waited for some moments. Not a word. She was looking fixedly at her handbag. I think she blushed a little. I didn't try to find out if the blush came from radiance or from shame. Then I pursued: "Considering my age and yours, the most logical thing would have been for me to keep my mouth shut; but I believe, in any case, that it was a homage that I owed to you. I'm not going to demand anything. If you, today or tomorrow or whenever, tell me to drop it, we won't say any more about it and will still be friends. And don't be afraid about the office, about being disturbed in your work; I'll behave, don't worry." I waited again. She was there, without defense—meaning defended only by me against myself. Whatever she was going to say, whatever attitude she was going to assume, would signify, "That is the color of your future." At the end I couldn't wait any longer and I said, "So?" With a smile that was somewhat forced, I added with a trembling voice that denied the jest it was supposed to be, "Have you anything to declare?" She stopped looking at her bag. When she raised her eyes, I could tell that the worst moment had passed. "I knew that," she said. "That's why I came to have coffee."

SATURDAY, MAY 18

Yesterday, when I was writing what she said to me, I didn't continue. I didn't go on because I wanted the day to finish in that way, with that upbeat of hope. She didn't say, "Stop." Not only didn't she say, "Stop," but she said, "That's why I came to have coffee." Afterward she asked me to give her a day, some hours at least, to think. "I knew it, and yet it's a surprise; I have to get over it." Tomorrow, Sunday, we're taking lunch at the Center. And now what? Actually my prepared speech had included a long explanation that I didn't even get to start on in the café. I wasn't at all sure that was the best way to proceed. I had also gone through the possibilities of offering myself as her counselor, to put the experience of my years at her disposition. However, when I came out of my financial calculations and found her in front of me, and fell into all those awkward and uncontrolled postures, then I got a dim notion of the truth. The only way out, the only fruitful escape from my absurd position, was to say what the inspiration of the moment would dictate, and no more, forgetting my prepared speeches and all the anticipated complications. I'm not sorry that I followed that impulse. My statement came out short and—above all—sincere, and I believe that sincerity will be the winning card in my game with her. I want to think so, that's for sure. But I ask myself, if she knew that I felt what I feel, how is it that she could vacillate in her own attitude? The explanations could be various. For example, she planned to pronounce the terrible "Please stop," but she found that it was too cruel to shoot that at me point-blank. Other explanation; that she had known ("known," in this case, means intuitively) how I felt, how I feel, but, notwithstanding, she hadn't believed that I'd come to expressing it in words, in a concrete proposition. Hence the vacillation. But she said it was "for that reason" that she came to take coffee. What does that mean? That she wanted me to pose that question—and in consequence to have the doubt? If one wants another to pose a question of that type, it is generally to respond in the affirmative. But also she might have wanted me to present the question finally, so as not to continue to wait for it, tense and uncomfortable; so as to be in a position, once and for all, to say no and to regain her equilibrium. Besides, there is her boyfriend, the ex-boyfriend. What's happening with him? Not as far as the facts are concerned (the facts, evidently, indicate that their relations have ended), but in herself. Would I provide, in concrete fashion, the impulse that she lacked, the little push that she was undoubtedly waiting for in order to return to him? But there are also the difference of age, my condition as widower, my three children, etc. And then I have to decide what type of relationship I'd want to maintain with her. The last is the most complicated part of the whole affair. If this diary were destined for a reader other than myself, I should close today's entry in the style of the serial novels: "If you want to know the answers to these pressing questions, read our next issue."

SUNDAY, MAY 19

I waited for her at Mercedes and Rio Branco Street. She arrived only ten minutes late. Her tailored suit, for Sundays, improved her appearance a lot, but it is probable that I was in the mood to find her looking better, always better. Today she was really nervous. Her little suit was a favorable sign (she wanted to make a good impression); her nervousness was not. I divined that beneath the rouge her cheeks and lips were pale. In the restaurant we chose a table at the back, almost hidden. "She doesn't want to be seen with me. A bad sign," I thought. Hardly had she sat down when she took out her mirror and looked at herself. "She's watching her appearance. Good sign." This time there was a half hour (while we ordered ham and the wine, while we spread butter on the black bread) during which the themes were general. Suddenly she said, "Please don't riddle me with those expectant looks. " "I don't have any others," I answered, like an idiot. "You want to know my answer," she added, "and my answer is another question." "Ask it," I said. "What does it mean, that you are in love with me?" It had never occurred to me that such a question existed, but here it was. It had caught up with me. "Please, Avellaneda, don't make me appear more ridiculous still. Do you want to be specific, like an adolescent, about what this being-in-love consists of?" "No, not at all." "Well, then?" In reality I was only acting. At bottom I knew quite well what she was trying to tell me. "So," she said, "you don't want to appear ridiculous, but you have no objection if I appear that way. To be in love can signify—especially in the language of you men—many different things." "You are right. Then give it the best of these many things. That's what I meant yesterday, when I said it." It wasn't a very hopeful dialogue of love. The verbal rhythm seemed to correspond to a conversation between business-men, or professors, or politicians, or any of those who possess self-control and equilibrium. "Look," I went on, with more animation, "there is what we call reality and there is what we call appearances." "Aha," said she, but not in a mocking tone. Then I said, "I love you in the area of reality, but the problems arise when I think of what are called appearances." "What problems?" she asked, and this time I believe she was really intrigued. "Don't make me say that I could be your father, or that you are as old as one of my children. Don't make me say that, for that's the key to all the problems; and saying it would make me feel pretty unhappy." She didn't answer. That was good; her silence carried the least risk. "Do you understand, then?" I asked, but I didn't wait for a response. "My object, apart from the very natural one of wanting to feel happy, is to try to make you feel happy too. And that's the difficult part. You have all that's needed to make my happiness, but I have very little to contribute to yours. And don't think that I've made up my mind about what place I should have in your life. Under other circumstances (I mean, rather, if other ages were involved) the correct thing would be to offer you a serious alliance—perhaps a too serious one—with a clear prospect of marriage within reach of your hand. But if I offered you that kind of thing it seems to me I would be very selfish, because I would be thinking only of myself, and what I now want the most is to think not of myself but of you. I can't forget—nor can you—that in ten years I'll be sixty. 'Hardly an old man,' an optimist or a flatterer would say, but the 'hardly' wouldn't change things much. I want to be honest enough to warn you that not now nor within a few months will I find the courage to talk matrimony. But—there's always a 'but'—what am I talking about then? Even if you understand the problem my way, it's still difficult to mention another arrangement. For in the other arrangement there is a place for love, but no place for marriage." She raised her eyes, but she didn't ask. Probably she only wanted to see my face as I said that phrase. But at this point I was decided not to hold back. "As for the other thing, popular imagination, which is usually poor in definitions, calls it an 'affair' or an 'arrangement,' and it is logical enough that it should scare you some. To tell the truth, I myself am scared, but only because I'm afraid that you will think I'm proposing an affair to you. However, I wouldn't be departing a hairsbreadth from my principle of sincerity if I told you that what I am seeking can be termed an accord, a kind of compromise between my love and your liberty. I know, I know. You're thinking that the reality is exactly the opposite; that what I'm seeking is your love and my liberty. You have every right to believe that, but please recognize that in my turn I have every right to risk everything on one card. And that one card is the confidence that you can have in me." At that moment we were waiting for dessert. The waiter finally brought the two cup custards, and I asked for the check. Immediately after the last mouthful, Avellaneda wiped her mouth vigorously with her napkin and looked at me smiling. The smile formed a pair of little rays at the corners of her lips. "I like you," she said.

MONDAY, MAY 20

The plan agreed on is absolute liberty. To get to know each other and see what happens, to let time pass and think it over again. There'll be no binding ties. There'll be no contracts. She is splendid.

TUESDAY, MAY 21

"The tonic is doing you good," Blanca told me at noon. "You're more animated, happier."

FRIDAY, MAY 24

There's a kind of game now at the office. The game of Boss and Assistant. The rule is not to get out of the rhythm, the normal habits, the routine. At nine in the morning I distribute the work, to Muñoz, to Robledo, to

Avellaneda, to Santini. Avellaneda is just another person on the list, one of those who put out their hands in front of my desk for me to give them their folders. There's the hand of Muñoz, wrinkled, with nails like claws; Robledo's hand, short, almost square; Santini's hand, with delicate fingers and two rings; and next to his, Avellaneda's hand, with fingers resembling Santini's, but feminine instead of effeminate. I've already told her that every time she approaches with the others, and puts out her hand, I place a gallant kiss (mentally, of course) on her slender and sensitive fingers. She says it can't be noted in my stony countenance. At times she's tempted, and tries to infect me with her uncontrollable desire to laugh, but I hold firm. So firm that Muñoz approached me this afternoon and asked if anything was the matter, since for some days he had observed that I was a little preoccupied. "Is it because of the trial balance that's due soon? Don't worry, chief. We'll get the books up-to-date before you know it. In other years we've been much more behind." What do I care about the trial balance? I almost laughed in his face. But I had to make believe. "Do you think we'll make it, Muñoz? Look, afterward the Excess Profits returns will be due and those tough guys will send back our affidavits two or three times, and then, of course, we'll get behind with our general work. We've got to put on pressure, Muñoz. Don't forget this is my last trial balance and I want it to come out right! Tell that to the boys, will you?"

SUNDAY, MAY 26

Today I dined with Vignale and Escayola. I must admit that it did something to me. I've never felt so severely the passage of time as I did today, when I sat opposite Escayola after thirty years of not seeing him, of knowing nothing about him. The tall, nervous joking adolescent has changed into a monstrous belly, with an impressive neck, white and fleshy lips, a baldpate with spots that look like dirty coffee, and some horrible bags beneath his eyes that pop out when he laughs. For Escayola laughs now. When he lived in Brandzen Street, the whole effect of his jokes came precisely from the fact that he told them very seriously. We all died laughing, but he remained impassive. At today's meal he made some jokes, told an off-color story that I've known since I went to college, and recounted some presumably piquant anecdote extracted from his experiences as a stock-exchange runner. The most he could accomplish was to get a moderate smile from me, while Vignale (really a dope) broke out in a fit of laughter so artificial that it sounded more like clearing his throat. I couldn't help saying to Escayola, "Apart from all those extra pounds you've put on, what I find strangest about you is that now you laugh so hard. Before, you made the most outrageous jokes with the face of an undertaker, and it was sensational." A glint of anger came into Escayola's eyes, or perhaps it was help-lessness, and straightaway he began to explain. "You know what has happened? I always made my jokes with a solemn face, you're right—how well you remember! But one day I noticed that I had run out of material. I never liked to repeat other people's stories. You know I used to be a creator. Any joke I told no one had ever told before. I invented them and at times I invented a whole series of funny tales with a central character, as in the comic strips, and I could use it for two or three weeks. But later, when I realized that I hadn't any themes of my own (I don't know what happened; all I can say is that my brain was emptied out), I didn't want to retire from the game at the right time, as a good sport should, so I began to repeat other people's jokes. At first I was very selective, but then I even got tired of choosing, and I added anything at all to my repertoire. And the people, the boys (I always had my public), began not to laugh; they didn't find anything I said to be funny. They were right, but still I didn't give up. I invented another procedure: to laugh myself while I was speaking, so as to impress my hearers and convince them that the story was really very humorous. At first they joined me in laughing, but soon they learned they were being cheated, that when I laughed I wasn't guaranteeing a really good joke. They were right about that too, but now I couldn't stop my laughing. And here I am, turned into a bore. Do you want some advice? If you want to keep my friendship, talk to me about tragic things."

TUESDAY, MAY 28

She comes nearly every day to take coffee with me. The general tone of our conversation is always that of friendship. At best, of friendship and something more. But I see progress being made in that "something more." For example, at times we speak of "Our Matter." Our Matter is the definite bond that now unites us. But when we mention it, it's always from the outside. Let me explain: we say, for example, "In the office no one notices Our Matter," or that such and such a thing happened before Our Matter began. But, actually, what is Our Matter? For now, at least, it's a kind of complicity, something against everyone else, a shared secret, a unilateral compact. Naturally, that isn't an "adventure" or an "affair," or—least of all—an engagement. However, it's something more than a friendship. The worst (the best?) about it is that she finds herself very comfortable in this indefinite state. She talks to me very frankly, with a lot of humor; I believe she goes as far as affection. She has a picture, a very personal and quite ironic one, of what's going on around her. She doesn't like to hear nasty stories about the office, but she has all the people well catalogued. At times, in the café, she looks about her, and she drops a remark that's well-placed, well-phrased, unimprovable. Today, for example, there was a table with four or five women, all of them about thirty to thirty-five. She looked at them attentively and then she asked me, "They're writers, aren't they?" In fact they were writers. I've known some of them, at least by sight, for some years. "Do you know them?" I asked. "No, I've never seen them before." "Well, then?" "I don't know; I can always recognize women who are writers. They have quite special features and habits, which you don't find in other professions. Either they paint their lips with a single hard line, as if they were writing on a blackboard, or their throats are always raspy from reading aloud so much stuff they write; and they can't lift their handbags, because of all the papers stuffed into them. They talk with restraint, as if they don't want to say anything against the legal code, and you'll never see them looking into a mirror. Imagine this—the second from the left has the calves of a champion athlete. And the one next to her looks as if she doesn't know how to fry an egg. They give me the creeps; how about you?" No, they don't give me the creeps; on the contrary, I recall a woman writer who is the proprietress of the most attractive bust in the universe and surrounding areas; but it amuses me to listen to Avellaneda when she gets excited about the pros or cons of some matter. The poor authoresses, masculine, energetic, muscular, kept on their discussion, entirely oblivious of the destructive critic who, over our table, kept adding new reproaches about their appearance, their posture, their attitude and their talk.

THURSDAY, MAY 30

The friend of Esteban is quite a guy. He wants 50 percent of my first retirement check. But he assures me that I won't have to work a single day more than is legally required. The temptation was great. It was indeed great, for I fell. He reduced it to 40 percent, and advised me to accept that before he changed his mind, for he never went that low with anyone; he never took less than 50 percent, but he'd do it this once only "because in my profession there are many crooks and unscrupulous people," and he was making this special price for me in order to do business with Esteban's father. "I love that skinny chap like a brother. During four years we played billiards every night. That unites people, mister." I remembered Aníbal, and our conversation of Sunday, May 5, when I said to him, "But now we also hand out bribes to be allowed to do something legal, and that means that all standards are gone."

FRIDAY, MAY 31

May 31 was Isabel's birthday. How far away it is! Once for her birthday I bought her a doll. It was a German doll, which moved its eyes and walked. I brought it home in a large box of thick cardboard. I put it on the bed and asked her to guess. "A doll," she said right off. I never forgave her for that.

None of the children remembered the date. At least, they said nothing about it to me. They have gradually gotten away from the cult of their mother. I believe that Blanca is the only one who even talks about her, who mentions her name in a natural way. Am I the one to blame for that? In the first years I didn't speak about her very much, solely because that gave me pain. Now I don't talk much about her either, because I'm afraid to make a mistake; I'm afraid of talking about some other person who has nothing to do with my wife.

Will the time come for Avellaneda to forget me? Here's the mystery: before one begins to forget, one has to remember, to begin to remember.

SUNDAY, JUNE 2

Time passes. At times I think I ought to live to the full, and extract the most from the years that remain. These days anyone could say to me, after examining my wrinkles, "But you're still a young man." Still. How many years of "still" are left for me? I think about that and a fear takes hold of me, the anguished sensation that my life is escaping, as if my veins have been opened and I can't keep my blood from flowing. Indeed, life is many things (work, money, luck, friendship, health, complications) but no one can deny that when we think of that word "life," when we say, for example, that we "cling to life," we are likening it to another word, more concrete, more attractive, more assuredly important. We are likening it to pleasure. I think about enjoyment (any form of enjoyment) and I am sure that that is life. Hence, the pressure, the tragic pressure of those fifty years that are treading on my heels. There still remain for me, I hope, some few years of friendship, of passable health, of routine emotions, of hoping for good luck, but how many of pleasure? When I was twenty years old I was young; at thirty I was young; at forty I was young. Now I'm fifty and I am "still young." "Still" means the end is near.

And that's the absurd side of our agreement. We say that we'll take things calmly, we'll let time pass, and then we'll review the situation. But time is running, whether we let it or not; time is running, and it makes *her* every day more appetizing, more mature, more lively, more a woman; but it threatens to make *me* every day more full of ailments, more infirm, less valiant, less vital. We shall have to hurry toward our full accord, because in our case the future is an inevitable disaccord. Each plus of hers corresponds to a minus of mine. Each of her minuses corresponds with a plus of mine. I understand that for a young woman it can be attractive to know that her friend is a person who has lived, who long ago exchanged his innocence for experience, who thinks with his head well set on his shoulders. But experience is good when there is a vigorous hand to grasp it; afterward, when the vigor departs, a man becomes a decorous museum piece, whose only value is as a record of what once existed. Experience and vigor exist together for a very little time. And now I am in that very little time. It's not an enviable lot.

TUESDAY, JUNE 4

Sensational. The Valverde girl has had a fight with Suárez. The whole office is turned upside down.

Martínez's face is a hymn. For him that break signifies, clearly and simply, the assistant managership. Suárez didn't come in this morning. He arrived in the afternoon, with a black eye, and the air of an undertaker. The manager called him in and gave him a dressing down. That means that we're not dealing with a mere rumor, but with an official and authorized version.

FRIDAY, JUNE 7

Up to now the two of us have been twice to the movies, but afterward she went back alone. Today, for a change, I accompanied her home. She had been very cordial, very companionable. In the middle of the film, when Alida Valli suffers so much from that imbecile Farley Granger, I felt suddenly that her hand was resting on my arm. I believe it was a reflex movement, but in any case she didn't withdraw it afterward. I have within me a gentleman who doesn't want to force events, but also there is another gentleman who is thinking obsessively of getting things going.

We got off the car at Eighth of October Street and we walked three blocks. It was dark, but it was the clear darkness of a night left to itself. The electric company, the old and wise UTE, made me a present of a blackout. She was walking apart from me, say three feet away. But when I came close to a corner (a corner with a bar, where a card table was lit up by candles), someone slowly separated his shadow from the shadow of a tree. The distance of a yard vanished, and before I knew it she was giving me her arm. The owner of the shadow was a drunk, an inoffensive and helpless drunk who murmured, "Long live the poor in spirit and the National Party!" I felt that Avellaneda was stifling a little laugh and that the tension of her fingers was relaxing. Her house is No. 368 on a street with a full name, something like Ramón P. Guitíerrez or Edurado Z. Domínguez, I don't remember exactly. It has an entrance vestibule and balconies. The door was closed, but she told me that there is a passage inside with something that aspires to be stained-glass windows. "They say the owner wanted to imitate the windows of Notre Dame, but I assure you there's a Saint Sebastian that looks just like Gardel."

She didn't open the door right away. She leaned gently against it. I thought that the bronze door handles were rubbing against her spine. But she didn't seem to mind. Then she said, "You're very good. I mean, you're behaving very well." But I, who know myself, lied like a saint: "Of course I am good, but I'm not sure that I'm behaving well." "I don't believe that," she said. "Didn't they teach you, when you were little, that when one behaves himself he doesn't have to recognize it?" That was the big moment, and she was waiting for what I was going to say. "When I was little they taught me that whenever one behaved well he received a reward. Don't I deserve one—perhaps?" There was an instant of silence. I couldn't see her face because the foliage of a damned pine tree cut off the moonlight. "Yes, you deserve it," I heard her say. Then her two arms emerged from the darkness and placed themselves on my shoulders. She must have seen this preliminary gesture in an Argentine movie. But the kiss that followed she hadn't seen in any film, that's sure. I like her lips—their taste, the way they sink against mine, the way they half open, the way they leave my mouth. Naturally, it wasn't her first kiss. What of it? After all, it's a relief to be able once more to kiss someone on the mouth with confidence and affection.

I don't know how it happened, I don't know what strange maneuver we made, but the one thing sure is that the bronze door handle was sticking into *my* spine. We spent a half hour at the door of No. 368. Lord, that was progress! Neither she nor I said it, but from this day on something has been established. Tomorrow I'll think about that. Now I'm tired. But I can also write: happy. Yet I'm too much on guard to call myself totally happy. On guard against myself, against fortune, against that only tangible future, which is called "tomorrow." On guard; that is to say, suspicious.

SUNDAY, JUNE 9

Perhaps I've a mania for equidistance. In every problem presented to me I'm never attracted by extreme solutions. That could be the root of my frustration. One thing is evident: if, on one side, extreme attitudes provoke enthusiasm, attract other people, are evidences of vigor; on the other side, middle-ground attitudes are in general inconvenient, at times disagreeable, and hardly ever seem heroic. Generally we need quite a lot of courage (a very special sort of courage) to hold ourselves in equilibrium, but still we can't avoid the consequences that to others it appears a demonstration of cowardice. Besides, the middle ground is boring. And to be boring is, in these days, the one inexcusable fault.

What does all this come to? Ah, yes. The equidistance that I am looking for now has to do (what doesn't have to do with her in my present life?) with Avellaneda. I don't want to hurt her and I don't want to hurt myself (first equidistance); I don't want our attachment to drag with it the absurdity of a formal engagement heading toward marriage, nor do I want it to take on the coloring of a vulgar, gross "affair" (second equidistance); I don't want the future to condemn me to being an old man despised by a woman in the fullness of her senses, nor do I want, from fear of such a future, to remain at the margin of this so attractive and irreplaceable a present (third equidistance); I don't want (fourth and final equidistance) to flit with her from furnished room to furnished room, and neither do I want to found a Home (with a capital letter).

Solutions? First: rent a little flat. Without abandoning my house, of course. Good, it's the first idea and the best. There isn't any other.

MONDAY, JUNE 10

Cold and wind. What a nuisance. To think that when I was fifteen I liked the winter. Now I begin sneezing and I lose count of how many times. I often have the sensation that in place of a nose I have a ripe tomato, with the ripeness that tomatoes have ten minutes before they begin to rot. When I reach the thirty-fifth sneeze I can't help feeling inferior to the rest of the human race. I wonder at the noses of the saints, those sharply cut and distinct noses that the saints of El Greco have, for example. I wonder at the noses of the saints, for they evidently were never chilled, and never cut to pieces by those endless chains of sneezes. Never. If they had sneezed in series of twenty or thirty consecutive explosions, they couldn't have avoided a like explosion of bad language, in thought if not in deed. And whoever uses bad language—even in its simplest form—thereby closes for himself the road to Glory.

TUESDAY, JUNE 11

I didn't tell her anything, but I've started in search of an apartment. I have an ideal one, all measured out in my head. Unfortunately, there are no bargain sales of ideal things; they always turn out to be dear.

FRIDAY, JUNE 14

It must be a month since I've had a conversation of more than five minutes with Jaime or Esteban. They come in grumbling, shut themselves up in their rooms, eat in silence while they read the paper, leave the house swearing, and come back at dawn. Blanca, on the contrary, is amiable, talkative, happy. I see very little of Diego, but I recognize his presence in Blanca's face. I haven't made a mistake; he's a good sort. Esteban has another political job. He arranged it at the club. I have the impression, however, that he has begun to be sorry that he's let himself be involved so completely. Someday he'll break out, I see it already, and send the whole thing to the devil. I hope it'll be soon. I don't like seeing him started on an enterprise that seems contrary to his old convictions. I don't like his becoming cynical, one of those cynics who, when the hour of accusation arrives, excuse themselves by saying: "It's the only way to get ahead, to become somebody." Jaime really does his work well; they like him at his job. But his problem lies somewhere else. The worst of it is that I don't know what it's all about. He's always nervous, dissatisfied. He seems to have character, but at times I'm not very sure if it's character or caprice. I don't like his friends. They have something of the good-for-nothing about them; they come from the Pocitos area and perhaps at bottom they look down on him. But they make use of him, because Jaime is skillful with his hands, and is always doing something they asked him to take care of. For nothing, as might be expected. None of them work; they are "father's boys." At times I hear them protest: "Jesus, your job is a pain in the neck. We can never count on you." They say "labor" for job, as if just to pronounce the word was an achievement; or like one of our Salvation Army men, who comes near a drunken beggar and, filled with disgust and piety, touches him with the point of his shoe; they say "labor" as if after they said it they would have to disinfect themselves.

SATURDAY, JUNE 15

I found an apartment. Near enough to my ideal, and unbelievably cheap. I'll have to stretch my budget anyway, but I hope it'll reach. The place is five blocks away from Eighteenth and Andes. It has the advantage, besides, that I can furnish it for peanuts. (They say that, but . . .) I'll just have to take out the balance of 2,466 pesos that I have at the Mortgage Bank.

Tonight I'm going out with her. I don't think I'll say anything.

SUNDAY, JUNE 16

However, I told her. We were walking the three blocks from Eighth of October Street up to her house, this time without a blackout. I believe that I began to stammer, trying to talk about our plan of absolute liberty, of seeing what would happen, of letting time run and then taking another look. I'm sure that I stammered. It's now a month since she appeared at Twenty-fifth and Missions to claim her coffee. "I want to propose something to you," I said. I have used the *tu* with her since Friday the 7th, but she doesn't do the same. I thought she was going to reply, "I know what it is," and that would have brought me much relief. But no. She left me to struggle with the entire burden. This time she didn't guess, or didn't want to guess. I was never a specialist in introductory remarks, so I limited myself to the indispensable: "I've rented an apartment. For us." It's too bad there wasn't a blackout, for in that case I wouldn't have seen her face. It was sad, perhaps. But how could I tell? I've never been very sure about what women mean when they look at me. At times I think they're asking me something, and after some time I realize that they are answering me. Between us two a word took its stand for a moment like a cloud, like a cloud that began to move. Both of us thought of the word "marriage," and both understood that the cloud was moving far off, that tomorrow the sky would be clear. "Without consulting me?" she asked. I answered yes by a nod. The truth was I had a knot in my throat. "It's OK," she said, trying to smile. "I'm a person you'll have to deal with that way, by the method of things already done." We were in the entrance. The outer door was unlocked because it was much earlier than the other day. There were lights here and there. It was no place for mystery. But there was something else, called silence. I began to understand that my proposition was not a perfect success. But at fifty one can't aspire to perfect successes. And if she had said no? For the fact that she hadn't said no

[85]

I was paying a price, and that price was the uncomfortable situation, seeing her silent in front of me, a little doubled up in her dark suit, with an expression of saying good-bye to various things. She didn't kiss me. And I didn't take the initiative, either. Her face was tense, harder-looking. Suddenly, without warning, it appeared that all her strength ebbed away, as if she had put off a mask she couldn't carry, and there as she was, looking upward, with the back of her neck against the door, she began to cry. And they weren't the romantic tears of happiness. It was the weeping that comes when one is sad and doesn't quite know why. When we feel unhappy for an evident reason, then it's natural and worthwhile to cry with the accompaniment of shakes, quakes and, above all, a public. But when, besides feeling unhappy, we feel in the dark, when there is no place for rebellion, for sacrifice or for heroism, then we must shed our tears noiselessly, because nobody can be of help and because we realize that the thing will pass and at the end we shall regain our equilibrium and a normal state. Her crying was like that. In that area no one can fool me. "Can I help you?" I said anyway. "Can I make things better somehow?" Silly questions. I produced another one, from the very bottom of my doubts: "What's the matter? Do you want to get married?" But the marriage cloud was far away. "No," she said. "I'm crying because it's just too bad." And that's right. Everything is too bad: that there wasn't a black-out, that I'm fifty years old, that she's a good kid, that I have three children, that there was this former boyfriend, that the apartment . . . I took out my handkerchief and wiped her eyes. "Is it all over now?" I asked. "Yes, it's all over." She was lying, but we both understood that it was good for her to lie. With her expression still not what it should be, she added, "Don't think that I'm always so silly." *"No creas,"* she had said; I'm sure she had said, *"No creas."* So she was using the *tu*.

THURSDAY, JUNE 20

I haven't written anything for four days. Between the arrangements for renting the apartment, their acceptance of the guarantee, the taking out of 2465.79 pesos, the purchase of some furniture, I've been in a fearful dither. Tomorrow they'll turn the apartment over to me. And Saturday afternoon the things will be delivered.

FRIDAY, JUNE 21

They let Suárez go. It's unbelievable, but they let him go. Everyone at the office is happily spreading the rumor that the Valverde girl brought pressure to have him fired. His Delivery Department made two errors in mailing. Suárez didn't even know about those mailings, which were certainly handled by one of those inexperienced youngsters who have the packaging job. In the not so distant past Suárez made quite a quantity of messy blunders and no one said anything. No doubt for the past three or four days the general manager must have had the order to get rid of this disgraced lover; but Suárez, who smelled what was coming, had been conducting himself like an exemplary child. He arrived on time; there were even days when he worked a short hour extra; he was amiable, humble, well-behaved. However, it didn't help him. If there hadn't been this mistake in Deliveries, I'm sure they would have dismissed him anyway, for smoking too much or for not having shined his shoes. Some sly chap maintains, on the other hand, that the packages were sent with a wrong address by the express and confidential order of the management. That wouldn't surprise me a bit.

When they gave Suárez the dismissal notice he was a sad sight. He went to the Cashier's Department, collected his indemnity, returned to his desk and began to empty the drawers in silence, with no one coming up to ask him what was happening, or to give him advice, or to offer to help him. In only half an hour he had become an undesirable. I hadn't spoken to him for years (since the day that I first discovered that he was taking confidential data from Accounting and transmitting them to one of the directors in order to poison him against the others) but I swear that today I felt a desire to come up to him and say some words of sympathy and advice. I didn't do it because the guy is as dirty as they come and didn't deserve what I wanted to do; but I couldn't help feeling a certain disgust before this sudden and total change, in which everyone participated, from the chairman of the board of directors down to the lowest messenger boy—based exclusively on the suspension of relations between Suárez and Valverde's daughter. It may seem strange, but the climate of this commercial enterprise was determined, in good part, by one person's orgasms.

SATURDAY, JUNE 22

I didn't go to the office. Taking advantage of the jubilant chaos of yesterday, I asked the manager if I could show up missing this morning. This he granted with smiles and even with the stimulating and humorous comment that he didn't know how he could get along without the key man of the office. Would they want to palm Valverde's daughter off on me? Bah.

I received the furniture in the apartment and I worked like a slave. It turned out well. Nothing madly modern. I don't like those functional chairs with such ridiculously unstable legs that they collapse if you do no more than give them an angry look. I don't like their backs, either, that always seem to be made to the measure of another user. I don't care for those lamps that always illuminate things one has no interest in viewing or showing—e.g., spider webs, cockroaches, electric fuses.

I believe this is the first time that I arranged an apartment to my taste. When I got married my family presented us with the bedroom and Isabel's family contributed the dining room. Each clashed with the other, but never mind. Then my mother-in-law came and laid down the law: You two need a little picture in the living room. She didn't have to say it twice. The next morning there appeared a still life, with sausages, hard cheese, a melon, rye bread, bottles of beer—a mess that in the end made me lose my appetite for six months. Other times, generally for wedding anniversaries, a certain uncle sent us engravings to hang on the wall of our bedroom, or two majolica vases with little effeminate-looking pageboys on them, that were repugnant as hell. After Isabel died, the passage of time, my various distractions and the vagaries of our domestics put a gradual end to the still lifes, the engravings and the little pages; but while that happened Jaime was filling the house with those crazy works of art that have to be continually explained. At times I saw them, he and his friends, in ecstasy before a jar that had painted on it wings, newspaper clippings, a door and testicles, and I heard them commenting, "What a barbarous reproduction!" I don't understand all this and don't want to understand; I'm sure that their admiration contains a lot of hypocrisy. Once I asked them, "Why don't you bring us someday something by Gauguin, or Monet, or Renoir? They're not bad, are they?" Then little Daniel Gómez Ferrando, a good-for-nothing who goes to bed every day at five in the morning "because the night hours are the most authentic," a sybarite who won't enter a restaurant after he sees someone there who uses toothpicks—this man, precisely he, answered me, "Because, sir, we are in the Abstract." But he, on his side, is nothing abstract, with his face without eyelashes and his eternal expression of a little pregnant cat.

SUNDAY, JUNE 23

I opened the door and stepped to one side to let her pass. She came in with short steps, looking at everything with close attention, as if she had wanted to absorb slowly the light, the atmosphere, the odor. She passed her hand over the book table, then over the upholstery of the sofa. She didn't even look at the bedroom. She sat down, tried to smile, but couldn't. It looked to me as if her legs were trembling. She gazed at the reproductions on the wall. "Botticelli," she said, making a mistake; it was Filippo Lippi. There will be time to enlighten her. She began to ask about quality, about prices, about furniture stores. "I like it," she said two or three times.

The sun, nearly set, changed to orange the cream-colored paper on the walls. I sat down beside her, and she became rigid. She hadn't even put down her handbag. I asked her, "Don't you remember that you're not a visitor, but the mistress of the house?" Then, making an effort, she fluffed up her hair a little, took off her jacket and nervously stretched her legs. "What's the matter?" I asked. "Are you scared?" "Do I look it?" She answered with a question. "Frankly, yes." "Could be. But it's not of you or me." "I know . . . you're scared of this moment." Then it seemed to me she quieted down. One thing was certain, she was not acting. Her paleness meant that her fear was real. Her behavior wasn't like that of those cash-register girls who agree to go to a furnished room, but who, at the moment that the taxi speeds off, become duly hysterical and emit loud cries of "Mama." No, there's nothing theatrical about her. She was confused, and I wouldn't want to investigate too deeply the causes of her confusion. "The point is that I have to accustom myself to the idea," she said, perhaps to reassure me. (She noticed that I was a little out of breath.) "One always imagines these things a little different from what they turn out to be later. But there's something I should recognize and thank you for. What you've arranged isn't too different from what I had thought about." "Since when?" "Since I went to high school and fell in love with the mathematics teacher." The table was ready, with those smooth yellow plates that the salesgirl at the bazaar had chosen for me. Not really that, for I liked them too. I served the ham, and discharged with all dignity my role as host. As for her, she liked everything, I'm sure, but the tension didn't allow her to enjoy any of it. When the moment came to uncork the champagne, she was no longer pale. "How long can you stay?" I asked. "Until late." "And your mother?" "Mother knows about Our Matter."

That was a blow below the belt. That's not permitted. I felt naked, with that desperate nudity of a dream, when one is walking around in shorts in the swank Sarandi area and people are enjoying the spectacle from one sidewalk to the other. "But why that?" I summoned up the courage to ask. "My mother knows everything about me." "And your father?" "Father lives outside the world. He is a tailor. And a terrible one. Never go to him for a suit. He makes them all to fit the same manikin. But, besides, he is a theosophist. And an anarchist. He never asks any questions. On Mondays he gets together with his theosophist friends and they discuss Madame Blavatsky until dawn; on Thursdays his anarchist friends come to our house and they shout arguments about Bakunin and Kropotkin. Otherwise he is a gentle, peaceful man, who looks at me with sweet patience and tells me a lot of useful things, the most useful things I have ever heard." I'm very pleased when she speaks of her family, but today I was especially pleased. It seemed to me that it was a good presage for the start of our intimate relations. "But your mother, what does she say about me?" "About you? Nothing. She talks about me." She finished the champagne remaining in her glass and wiped her lips with the paper napkin. Now no lipstick was left. "She says about me that I'm an extremist, that I don't have serenity." "With respect to Our Matter or with respect to everything?" "Everything. Her theory, the great theory of her life, the one that keeps her going, is that true happiness is much less angelic and quite a bit less agreeable than what we tend to dream. She says that people finish up generally by feeling unhappy, for no other reason than because they had believed that happiness was a permanent sensation of indefinable well-being, of ecstatic enjoyment, of perpetual feasting. No, she says, happiness is something a good deal less (or perhaps a good deal more, but in any case something else), and she's sure that many of those who consider themselves unhappy are in reality quite happy; but they're not aware of it, they don't admit it, because they believe that they are very far away from the acme of well-being. It's something like what happens to those who are disappointed with the Blue Grotto. What they imagined was a grotto of fairies, without knowing just what to expect. It really is a fairy grotto, but when they get there they find that the miracle consists only of putting one's hands in the water and seeing them slightly blue and luminous." Evidently she enjoys recounting the reflections of her mother. I think she tells each of them as a conviction unattainable by her, but also as one she would fervently love to possess. "And you, how do you feel?" I asked. "As if you saw your hands turn slightly blue and luminous?" The interruption brought her back to earth, to the special moment that was this Today. "Anyway, we are putting them in the water," she said, but then she blushed. For clearly that sentence could be taken for an invitation, even for an urgent demand, that she hadn't wanted to formulate. That wasn't my fault, but it turned out to be a bad break for me. She got up, leaned against the wall and asked me in a tone that she wanted to sound sympathetic, but which in reality was all too inhibited, "Can I ask you a first favor?" "You can," I said, and now I was worried. "Will you let me leave, like this, without anything else?" I felt disappointed, imbecile, understanding. "Of course I'll let you go." As if I could do anything else. But I could have done something else. How I could have done something else!

Esteban is sick. The doctor says it could be a serious affair. Let's hope not. Pleurisy or something else in the lungs. He doesn't know. When will the doctors know? After lunch I went into his room to see how he was. He was reading with the radio on. When he saw me come in he closed the book, after turning down the upper corner of the page he was reading. He turned off the radio. As if to say, "Well, my private life is over for now." I acted as if I didn't notice those things. I didn't know what to talk about. I never know what to talk about with Esteban. Whatever theme we touch, we are fated to end in an argument. He asked me how my retirement was getting on. I think it's getting on all right. In reality it can't be too complicated. Some time ago I arranged my part of the program, I paid the necessary contributions and put my official record in order. "According to your friend, the affair won't take long." The subject of retirement is one of the most frequent between Esteban and me. We have a sort of tacit agreement to keep it always up to date. Nevertheless, today I made a different try: "Well, tell me a little about how your affairs are going. We never talk." "That's true. It must be because both you and I are always very busy." "That may be. But do you really have much to do at the office?" An idiotic question, the kind one asks of a saleslady. The reply was the predictable one, but I hadn't foreseen it. "What do you mean? That public employees are always lazy? Sure, only you, the honorable employees in private business, have the right to be efficient and hard workers." I felt doubly angry, because it was my fault.

"Look, don't be stupid. I didn't mean that and I didn't even think it. You're as touchy as an old maid." I had no right to hope for it, but I didn't offend him. The fever must have weakened him. More than that, he even made excuses. "You may be right. I'm always in bad humor. I don't know, it's as if I felt uncomfortable with myself." As a confession, and coming from Esteban, it was almost too much. But as self-criticism, I believe it very close to the truth. For a long time I've had the impression that Esteban's conduct doesn't accord with his conscience. "What would you say if I left government service?" "Now?" "Well, not now. When I get better, if I get better. The doctor says that at best I'll be ill for several months." "And what's the reason for this change of heart?" "Don't ask me too much. Aren't you satisfied that I want to change?" "Of course I'm satisfied. You make me very happy. The one thing that bothers me now is that if you want to take sick leave it's easier to get it where you are now." "And you—when you had typhoid, did they fire you? Of course not. And you were absent about six months." Actually, I had taken the other side for the pleasure of hearing him stick to his decision. "The most important thing now is for you to get better. After that we'll see." Then he launched on a long picture of himself, of his limitations and his hopes. It was so long that I got back to the office at three-fifteen, and I had to give my excuses to the manager. I had been impatient about that while Esteban talked, but I didn't feel I had the right to interrupt him. It was the first time the boy had taken me into his confidence. I couldn't cut him short. After he finished I talked to him. I gave him some advice, but very general, and to no special effect. I didn't want to frighten him. And I believe that I didn't frighten him. When I left

I squeezed his knee, which projected under the covers. And he sent me a smile. Heavens, he seemed to have the face of a stranger. Could that be possible? On the other hand, a very sympathetic stranger. And he is my son. That's good.

I had to stay late at the office and consequently I had to postpone the start of my "honeymoon."

TUESDAY, JUNE 25

Worked my head off. It will be for tomorrow.

WEDNESDAY, JUNE 26

I had to work until 10 P.M. I'm literally a wreck.

THURSDAY, JUNE 27

I believe that today must have been the last of the terrible rush. I've never seen a more complicated and more useless request for information. And we still have the trial balance ahead of us.

Esteban is over his fever. He's not as sick as he was.

FRIDAY, JUNE 28

At last. At six-thirty I left the office and went to the apartment. She had arrived before me, had opened it with her key and installed herself. When I came in she received me happily, without inhibitions, and once more with a kiss. We ate. We talked. We laughed. We made love. Everything went so well that I just can't describe it. I'm praying, "May it only last," and to put pressure on God I'm going to knock a special kind of wood.

It appears that Esteban's trouble isn't so serious. The X rays and the analyses contradicted the doctor's gloomy prophecy. This type likes to terrify us, to announce that grave complications are around the corner, with indefinite and implacable dangers. Afterward, if the reality isn't so fearful, a great sensation of relief supervenes, and the relief felt by the family is ordinarily the best possible climate for paying without complaint, even with gratitude, an outrageously high bill. When we ask the doctor for that bill, humbly, with embarrassment, feeling clearly the poor taste of touching on so vulgar and gross a subject in front of someone who is sacrificing his life and his time for the salvation of his neighbor: "How much is it, doctor?" he always says, accompanying his words with a generous and comprehensive gesture of unease: "Please, friend, there'll be time to talk about that. And don't worry, that will never be a problem with me." And right away, to rescue our human dignity from that sordid pitfall, he puts a stop to that conversation and starts giving pontifical orders about the little bouillon that the convalescent will take tomorrow. Later, when finally the time comes "to talk about that," the inflated bill arrives, all alone, by post, and we are left a bit dazed by the figures, perhaps because at that moment we are not being treated to the affable, paternal, Franciscan smile of that austere martyr to science.

SUNDAY, JUNE 30

A whole day for us, from breakfast on. I arrived in an anxious state, to verify, to prove everything. What had happened on Friday was a unique thing, but flood-like. Everything went so fast, so naturally, so happily, that I couldn't take a single mental note. When one is in the very focus of life, it is impossible to reflect. And I want to reflect, to measure as closely as possible this strange thing that is happening to me, to recognize my own signals, to compensate for my lack of youthfulness by my excess of consciousness. And among the details that I want to verify is the tone of her voice, the shades of her voice, from extreme sincerity to ingenuous artifice. There is her body, which virtually I didn't see, which I couldn't discover, because I preferred deliberately to pay that price, feeling that her tenseness was thereby diminished, that her nerves were ceding to her sensations; I preferred that the darkness be truly impenetrable, proof against every fissure of light, so that her quiverings of shame, of fear, of whatnot should gradually be changed into other quiverings, softer, more normal, more suited to her surrender. Today she said to me, "I'm happy about everything that happened." And it seemed, by the emphasis of her words, by the light in her eyes, that she might be referring to a medical examination, a childbirth, an attack of illness, to anything of greater risk and responsibility than the simple, current, daily operation of a man and *his* woman sleeping together—which is much more simple, current and everyday than that of a man and *a* woman sleeping together. "Even so far as to say that I feel without fault, clean of any sin." I must have made an impatient gesture, because she added right away, "I know that you can't understand that; it's something that doesn't fit within the several fingerbreadths of a masculine forehead. For you men, making love is a sort of normal procedure, almost an obligation of hygiene, seldom a case for the conscience. I envy how you can separate this detail called sex from all the other essentials, the other zones of life. You men have invented the idea that sex is everything in a woman. You invented it, and afterward disfigured it; you converted it into a caricature of what it really signifies. When you say that you think of woman as an impenitent enjoyer of sexual love who follows it as her vocation, that 'sex is everything in a woman,' you mean that her entire life, including her adornments, her arts of attraction, her varnish of culture, her quick tears—all that is her equipment of seduction to catch a man and convert him into the provider of her sexual life, her sexual needs, her sexual rites." She seemed excited and almost angry at me. She looked at me with an irony so assured that she appeared to be the depositary of all the feminine dignity of this world. "And nothing of that is correct?" I asked, wanting only to provoke her, for her aggressive posture made her look very pretty. "Some of it is right, it's right at times. I know there are women who are like that and nothing more. But there are others, the majority, who are not that way, and still others who, even if they are that way, are something else besides: human beings—complicated, egocentric, extremely sensitive. Perhaps it is true that the feminine ego is synonymous with sex, but you must understand that a woman identifies sex with conscience. That joining can produce the greatest sin, the best happiness, the most difficult problem. But for you it's so different. Compare, if you please, the case of a single girl and a bachelor, two persons who in appearance would seem to be closely similar, with parallel frustrations. What are the reactions of one and the other?" She took breath and continued.

"While the single girl turns into an old maid—in bad

humor, continually less feminine, paranoid, hysterical, incomplete—the bachelor on the other hand turns outward, becomes amusing, noisy, an old buck. They both suffer from solitude; but for the bachelor being alone is nothing but a problem of domestic help, or sleeping in a single bed; while for the old maid her solitude is a mallet blow on her head." It was most inopportune on my part, but at that moment I laughed. She stopped her speech and looked at me inquiringly. "I'm amused to hear you defend the old maids," I said. "I like that, and besides, it surprises me to see you at such pains to formulate your theory. You must inherit that from your mother. She has her theory of happiness; you too have yours, which can be denominated: 'On the connections between sexuality and conscience in the average woman.' But now tell me, where did you find that we men think in that fashion, that it was men who invented this foolishness that sex is everything for a woman?" She took on an ashamed expression, knowing herself cornered. "What do I know? Somebody told me that. I'm not erudite. But if men hadn't invented that notion, they deserve the charge of inventing it." Now indeed I could recognize her, in that escape of a little girl who sees she is found out and turns to a trick of apparent naïveté to get herself excused. After all, I'm not bothered much by her feminist outbursts. She really said all that to explain to me why she had ceased to feel guilty. Good, that's the important thing, that she shouldn't believe herself at fault, that the tension should diminish, that she should feel comfortable in my arms. The rest is trimmings, justification; it can be true or not, it's all the same to me. If she likes to feel herself justified, if she converts all this into a grave problem of conscience, if she wants me to understand it, if

I must listen to her talk about it—OK, let her talk and I'll listen. She looks very lovely, with her cheeks all aflame from excitement. Besides, I'm not so sure that it isn't a question of conscience for me too. I don't know what day I wrote it, but I'm sure that I made a record of my vacillations, and what is vacillation but a bout of conscience?

But she's a wonder. Suddenly she stopped talking, put aside all her militancy and looked at herself in the mirror, not with coquetry but as if making fun of herself. She sat down on the bed and called to me: "Come, sit here, I'm an idiot to lose time making a speech like that. All in all, I know that you are not like the others. I know that you understand me, that you see the reason why my conscience is really involved in this." I had to lie and say, "Of course, I see it." But by now she was in my arms and she had other things to think about, other old projects to realize, other new caresses to await. Even the cases of conscience have their amorous side.

WEDNESDAY, JULY 3

It sounds incredible, but I haven't seen Aníbal since just after he returned from Brazil at the beginning of May. Yesterday he called me, and said he was all right. But he needed to talk and confide in somebody. Only then did I notice that I had kept the Avellaneda matter entirely to myself, without speaking about it to a soul. That's easy to understand. With whom could I have discussed it? With my children? Even to imagine that gives me gooseflesh. With Vignale? I can picture his malicious leer, his pat on the shoulder, his haw-haw of complicity, and immediately I turn away from the thought. With the fellows at business?

It would be a horrible faux pas, and at the same time it would make it absolutely certain that Avellaneda would have to leave the office. But even if she weren't working there I think that I wouldn't feel like talking about myself in that atmosphere. In offices there aren't any friends; there are fellows who see each other every day, who get angry separately or together, who crack jokes and laugh at them themselves, who exchange complaints and communicate their peeves, who swear at the board of directors in general and pay fulsome compliments to each director individually. This is called getting-along-together, but only by a mirage could it come to appear as friendship. In so many years at the office I confess that Avellaneda is the only one who has aroused a true emotion in me. The others are disqualified by a relationship which doesn't exist by choice; it's a bond imposed by circumstances. What do I have in common with Muñoz, with Méndez, with Robledo? Yes, at times we laugh together. We have a drink, we treat each other with a certain sympathy. At bottom each of us is unknown to the rest; for in this type of superficial relationship we talk of many things, but never of the vital ones, never of those that are truly important in our lives. I believe that work is the thing that gets in the way of true confidences; work is a sort of constant hammering, or like a poison gas. At times one of them (Muñoz especially) has come up to me to start a conversation that might really communicate something. He has begun to talk, begun to draw his self-portrait with frankness, begun to put together the terms of his drama, of that ordinary, banal, disconcerting drama that erodes the life of each one of us, the more we think of ourselves as average men. But then there's always someone calling Muñoz at the counter. For half an hour he has to explain to a bad-humored client why things have been delayed; he argues, yells a little and surely feels himself morally lowered. When he comes back to my desk he looks at me and says nothing. He makes the muscular effort corresponding to a smile, but the corners of his lips fold downward. Then he takes an old file cover, crushes it in his fist and throws it in the wastebasket. It's a simple substitute; what has no further use, what is thrown in the basket, is his confidential story. Yes, work interferes with mutual confidences.

But besides that, there are the office tricks. We are all specialists in jokes. The fact that our neighbors are available for our attention has to be made use of in some fashion; otherwise, being surrounded by them would work like a kind of cyst, and bring on claustrophobia, neurasthenia or whatever. Since we don't have enough courage or frankness to interest ourselves in a truly friendly way in our neighbor (not the Biblical neighbor, nebulous, faceless, but the neighbor with a first and last name, the neighbor nearest to us, he who is writing on the desk in front of mine, he who hands me his calculation of interest accrued, for me to look over and initial); since we voluntarily abstain from such friendship—that being so, we are going to interest ourselves in playing tricks on this neighbor who is vulnerable to them for eight hours every day. Furthermore, playing tricks establishes a sort of solidarity. Today the candidate is this one, tomorrow that one, the day afterward it will be me. The victim curses a bit in silence, but soon resigns himself, knowing that the joke played on him is just a part of the game, that in the near future, even within one or two hours, he will be able to choose the form of revenge that best coincides with his talents. The jokesmiths, for their part, feel united, enthusiastic, full of fun. Every time one of them adds some new condiment to the trick, the others celebrate, make signs to one another, feel a sensual thrill of complicity; all that's missing is that they should embrace and shout, "Hurray!" And what a relief it is to laugh, even when one has to muffle the laughter because in back of us the manager has put a scowl on his watermelon face; what a revenge it is against the routine, against the paper work, against that sentence to hell which consists of being entangled for eight hours in something that swells the bank account of those useless people who sin by the mere fact that they're alive, those inane people who believe in God solely because they don't realize that long ago God ceased to believe in them. Playing tricks and working. How are they different, after all? What work these jokes give us, what weariness! And what a silly trick is the work we do, what a bad joke!

THURSDAY, JULY 4

I talked for a long time with Aníbal. It's the first time that I pronounced the name of Avellaneda before anyone, that is to say, the first time I pronounced it with the feeling that this name belongs to me. For a time, while I told him the story, I seemed to see myself regarding the whole business from the outside, as a deeply interested spectator. Aníbal listened to me with concentrated attention. "But why don't you get married? I don't really understand the fine points of that scruple." It seemed unbelievable to me that he didn't understand; the reasons were so clear. I went back to my explanation, the same old explanation that I have been giving myself since the beginning: my age, her age, myself in ten years, her in ten years, my anxiety not to hurt her future, my other anxiety not to appear ridiculous, the thing being so enjoyable as it is, my three children, etc., etc. "And you figure that in this way you are not hurting her future?" Of course, some hurt is inevitable, but in every respect I am hurting her less than by chaining her to me. "And what does she say? Does she agree?" I call that an uncomfortable question. I don't know if she agrees. When I gave her the chance, she said yes, but truly I don't know if she agrees. Could it be that she would prefer the stable situation, officially established and consecrated? I said I was doing this for her, but could I have been doing it really for myself? "Are you afraid of being ridiculous or of something else?" Evidently the chap had his finger on the sore. "What do you mean by that?" "You asked me to be frank, didn't you? I mean that the whole problem is very clear to me: what's happening to you is that you're afraid that within ten years she'll be unfaithful to you." What an ugly thing it is for someone to tell you the truth, above all if it's one of the truths that you have avoided even in those early-morning soliloquies when you have just waked up and you are murmuring certain strange things as you go about taking off your pajamas—bitter things, things deeply hostile, charged with self-rancor, ideas that must be dissipated before you can wake up entirely and put on the mask that, for the rest of the day, other people will see and that will look at other people. So I am afraid that within ten years she will cheat on me? I answered Aníbal with a dirty word, which is the traditional male reaction when somebody talks about his wife cheating, even though the event may be long in the future. But the doubt went on turning in my head, and in this moment when I write about it I can't help feeling myself less generous, less well-adjusted, a little more vulgar and sour.

SATURDAY, JULY 6

It has rained buckets since noon. We stayed at a corner for twenty minutes, hoping that the thing would stop, gazing with discouragement at the people running. But we were getting a chill and I began to sneeze with a threatening regularity. It was just impossible to find a taxi. We were within two blocks of the apartment and we decided to walk there. In reality we ran like crazy, and we got to our place in three completely drenching minutes. For a while I felt terribly tired and I slumped on the bed like a useless article. But before that I had found the strength to look for a woolen blanket and to wrap her in it. She had taken off her jacket, which was dripping, and also her skirt, which was a mess. Little by little I came to myself and in half an hour I felt warm. I went to the kitchen, lit the primus, put on water to boil. From the bedroom she called me. She had gotten up and, enveloped in her blanket, she was next to the window, watching it rain. I came close to her, and I too watched how it rained; we didn't say anything for a while. All at once I realized that this moment, this tiny slice of daily life, was the culmination of well-being; it was happiness. I had never been so completely happy as at that moment. But I had the wounding sensation that it would never return, at least not with that intensity. A summit is like that, it has to be that way. Moreover, I am sure that the summit of happiness lasts only a second, a short second, a momentary illumination, and no one has the right to prolong it.

Down there a dog was trotting along, in no hurry, wearing a muzzle, resigned to what couldn't be helped. All at once he stopped, and obeying a canine inspiration, raised a leg, after which he continued his tranquil trot. It really looked as if he had stopped to make sure that it was still raining. We watched for a while and burst out laughing. I imagined that the spell had broken, that the so-called high point had been passed. But she was with me; I could feel her there, touch her, kiss her. I could say simply, "Avellaneda." "Avellaneda" is more than Avellaneda; it's a world of words. I am learning to inject hundreds of meanings into the name, and she is learning to recognize them. It's a game. In the morning I say, "Avellaneda," and that means, "Let's make love." She answers gaily, "Do you think I should leave now? It's so early!" Oh, those former days when Avellaneda was only a woman's name, the name of a new assistant (it's only five months since I wrote, "The girl doesn't seem overeager to work, but at least she understands what one explains to her"); it was the label to identify that little person with the wide forehead and large mouth who looked at me with enormous respect. Here she was now, opposite me, wrapped in her blanket. I can't remember how she was when she appeared insignificant, inhibited, a likable girl and no more. I remember only how she is now: a delicious little woman, who attracts me, who brings an absurd joy to my heart, who has conquered me completely. I blinked my eyes on purpose, so that nothing should be disturbed afterward. Then my glance enveloped her, much closer than her blanket; in reality my look was not separate from my voice, which had already begun to say, "Avellaneda." And this time she understood me perfectly.

A day of splendid sun, almost autumnal. We went to Carrasco. The beach was deserted, perhaps because in full July people haven't the courage to believe in good weather. We sat down on the sand. This way, with the beach empty, the waves become imposing; it is they alone that control the landscape. In this kind of thing I know I am too easily influenced by my surroundings. I gaze at this implacable and desolate sea, so proud of its foam and its might, scarcely flecked by the silly, almost unreal seagulls, and straightway I take refuge in an unconditional admiration. But almost immediately afterward, my admiration is changed into fear and I begin to feel myself as defenseless as a clam or a rolling stone. That sea is a kind of eternity. When I was a child it beat and it beat, but it also was beating when my grandfather was a child, when my grandfather's grandfather was a child. A presence that moves, but without life. A presence of waves, dark and insensible. Witness of history, but a useless witness since it knows nothing of history. And if the sea were God? Still an insensible witness. A presence moving, but without life. Avellaneda too was gazing, with the wind in her hair, almost without blinking. "Do you believe in God?" she asked, as if to continue the dialogue I had begun between myself and my thought. "I don't know. I would like God to exist. But I'm not sure. Nor am I sure that God, if he exists, would conform with our beliefs about him; they're all based on scattered and incomplete information." "But it's so clear. You complicate the matter because you want God to have a face, hands, a heart. God is a common denominator. We could also call him The Totality. God is this stone, my shoe, that seagull, your trousers, that cloud, everything." "And that idea appeals to you? Are you satisfied with it?" "At least it inspires me with respect." "To me, no. I can't imagine God as a huge stock company."

MONDAY, JULY 8

Esteban is up now. His illness left us with a good result, as much for him as for me. We have had two or three frank and truly beneficial conversations. We also talked about generalities now and then, but in a natural fashion, without having the answers dictated by our old incompatibility.

TUESDAY, JULY 9

"So I'm afraid that within ten years she'll be cheating on me?"

WEDNESDAY, JULY 10

Vignale. I met him in Sarandi. I couldn't get out of listening to him. He didn't seem happy. I was in a hurry, so we took our coffee at the counter. Here, at the top of his voice, in that style of stentorian confidence that he cultivates, he recounted to me the new chapter of his idyll. "What a tough situation. Listen. My wife is on to us, get it? She didn't find us in what they call *flagrante*. We were only kissing. But you can imagine the stink my fat spouse raised. In her own house, under her own roof, eating her own bread. I, who am her own husband, felt like a cockroach. Elvira, on the other hand, took it all with great calm, and invented the theory of the century: that she and I have always been like brother and sister and what my wife had seen was just that, a brotherly-sisterly kiss. I felt like an incestuous brute, and then fatty really started to carry on. 'You're pretty simple,' she shouted, 'if you think I'm going to be sweet and gentle like that poor nothing of a Francisco.' She spoke to my mother-in-law, the neighbors, the shopkeeper. At 2 P.M. the whole neighborhood knew that that little thing had wanted to steal her husband. On her side, Elvira talked vigorously with Francisco, and told him that she was being insulted and that she wouldn't stay in that house for another minute. However, she did stay there about three hours, during which she played a dirty trick on me. You can figure that Francisco was saying yes to everything; there was no danger coming from that direction. But my fat one kept on insisting and yelling, and once or twice she physically attacked Elvira. And then Elvira, in one of those moments of terror—can you imagine what she said? How could it enter anyone's head that she would pay any attention to a complete mess like me? Do you get it? And the worst was that by saying that she convinced my wife, and fatty calmed down. I swear to you that I'll never forgive Elvira for that. Let her get out, her and her husband with his horns. After all, look, she's not as nice as she seemed to me before. Furthermore, now that I've stopped being a faithful husband I've come to the conclusion that I can have little affairs with younger and fresher girls; above all, they won't have anything to do with my home life, which was always sacred to me. And at the same time my fat spouse won't be bothered."

She's at my side, fallen asleep. I'm writing on a separate sheet; tonight I'll transcribe this in my little book. It's 4 P.M., the end of the afternoon. I began to think of one comparison and I finished with another. Here, next to me, is her body. Outside it's cold, but here the temperature is agreeable; it's even hot. Her body is almost uncovered; the blanket and the sheet have slid to one side. I wanted to compare that body with my recollections of Isabel's body. Evidently those are of quite different experiences. Isabel wasn't slender, her breasts were filled out, and for that reason they sagged a little. Her navel was deep, large, dark, with thick edges. Her hips were the best, the part that attracted me the most; I have a tactile memory of her hips. Her shoulders were plump, of a rosy white. Her legs were threatened by a varicose future, but they were still lovely, well-turned. This body now at my side hasn't a single trait in common with the other. Avellaneda is skinny, her bust inspires me with a bit of pity, her shoulders are full of freckles, her navel is infantile and little; her hips too are the best feature (or is it that hips always make a great impression on me?), her legs are slender but they're well-made. However, the other's body attracted me and this one attracts me. In Isabel's nudity there was an inspiring force; I contemplated her and everything in me became sex, there was no reason to think of anything else. But in Avellaneda's nudity there is a sincere, unprotected and appealing modesty, a helplessness that is really moving. She attracts me deeply, but here sex provides only a part of the suggestion that makes me take fire. Isabel's nakedness was a total nakedness, perhaps purer on that account. To love Isabel it was enough to feel myself drawn by her body. Avellaneda's body combines nakedness with an attitude. To love Avellaneda it is necessary to love her nudity plus her attitude, since the second is at least half of her attractiveness. To hold Isabel in my arms meant to embrace a body sensitive to all the physical reactions and capable also of giving all the permitted stimulations. To hold in my arms the slenderness of Avellaneda means to embrace also her smile, her glance, her way of talking, the repertory of her tenderness, her hesitance to surrender completely and her excuses for her reticence. Well, that's the first comparison.

Then came the second comparison, and this one left me gray and dispirited. My own body in Isabel's time versus my present body for Avellaneda. What a melancholy thought. I've never been an athlete, God forbid! But then I had muscles, I had strength, then I had a smooth, taut skin. And above all I did not have many other things that unhappily I now possess. From the uneven baldness (the left side is the most barren), the broader nose, the warty neck, to my chest with islands of red hair, my sagging stomach, my varicose ankles, my incurable, depressing athlete's foot. As regards Avellaneda it's not so important; she knows me like this, she doesn't know how I used to be. But it's important for me; it means a lot to recognize myself as a phantom of my youth, as a caricature of myself. Perhaps there is a compensation: my head, my heart— in fine, myself as a spiritual being, perhaps all that is today a little better than it was in the days and nights with Isabel. Only a little better; it's not proper to have too many illusions about it. Let's be balanced, let's be objective. Let's be sincere, hang it! The ready-made answer is, "Does that count for anything?" God, if he exists, must be up there *"haciendo cruces"*. Avellaneda (thank God, she does exist), is now here below opening her eyes.

MONDAY, JULY 15

When all's said and done, Aníbal may be right that I'm avoiding marriage more from fear of ridicule than to protect Avellaneda's future. And that wouldn't be right. For one thing is sure, and that is that I love her. I write that just for myself, so it isn't important how it might sound to others. It's the truth. Period. By the same token, I don't want her to suffer. I believed (in reality I thought I believed) that I was avoiding a marriage situation in order that Avellaneda should always be free, to make sure that, after a few years, she should not feel herself chained to an old man. If it now appears that that was only a pretext, while the true reason was a sort of insurance against being deceived in the future, then it's pretty clear that I'll have to change the whole structure of this union. Perhaps she would suffer more from a clandestine, and always provisional, situation, than from feeling herself anchored to a fellow twice her age. In my fear of being ridiculous I was undoubtedly judging her wrong, and that was a base trick on my part. I know she's made of good stuff. If the time ever came when she fell in love with someone else, she would not leave me in that humiliating ignorance that constitutes the true insult to the one who loses out. If she should tell me first, then I hope that in some way I would acquire the serenity needed to understand. But perhaps it would be better to talk to her about it, to let her decide for herself, to help her feel secure n the way she finds best.

Blanca was sad today. Jaime, she and I ate in silence. Esteban was making his first nocturnal sally since his illness. I didn't say anything during dinner, for I know only too well how Jaime reacts. Afterward, when he left, virtually without saying good-bye (I couldn't take for "good night" the grumble that preceded the slamming of the door), I was reading the paper in the dining room. Blanca dallied on purpose while she was clearing the table. I had to raise the newspaper while she was taking off the cloth, and then I looked at her. Her eyes were wet. "What's happening with you and Jaime?" I asked her. "It's with Jaime and with Diego; I've had a fight with both of them." That was too much of a puzzle. I couldn't imagine Jaime and Diego allied against her. "Diego says that Jaime is a fairy. That's why I had a fight with Diego." The word "fairy" hit me twice: why was it directed at my son, and why had it been said by Diego, in whom I had placed my hopes, in whom I had such confidence? "And do you know for what reason your fine Diego allows himself to offer insults?" Blanca gave me a slightly bitter smile. "That's the worst. It isn't an insult. It's the truth. And that's why I had a fight with Jaime." It was evident that Blanca had a hard time saying all those words, especially since the revelation was being made to me. I didn't sound honest to myself when I replied, "And you give more credit to that lie of Diego's than to what your brother says." Blanca dropped her eyes. She was the image of a pathetic, pitiable creature.

"That's the point," she said. "Jaime admits it." Until that moment I would never have thought that my eyes could open that wide. My temples were hurting. "So it's those friends . . ." I stammered. "Yes," she said. It was a blow from a club. However, I recognized that a suspicion had already been planted in my inmost heart. For that reason the word didn't sound entirely new to me. "I ask you one thing," she added. "Don't say anything to him. He's a lost soul. He doesn't feel any scruples, can you imagine that? He says that women don't attract him, that it's something he didn't go looking for, that each of us has the nature God gave him, and that God didn't give him the capacity of feeling himself attracted by women. He defends himself strongly; I assure you he has no guilt complex." Then I said, without any conviction, "If I bash his head in, you'll see how he'll get a guilt complex." Blanca laughed for the first time that night. "Don't try to fool me. I know that you're not going to do that." Then I felt discouraged, horribly discouraged, without a shred of hope. This had to do with Jaime, with my son, the one who inherited Isabel's forehead and mouth.

Up to what point was it my fault, and where did his begin? I know that I didn't watch over them as I should have, that I couldn't take a mother's place completely. Alas, I wasn't built to act like a mother. I'm not even sure that I'm built to act like a father. But what has that to do with the way he has turned out? Perhaps I could have cut off those friendships when they began. Perhaps if I had done so he would have continued to see them without my knowing it. "I must speak to him," I said, and Blanca seemed to resign herself to the coming storm. "And besides, you'll have to make things up with Diego," I added.

THURSDAY, JULY 18

I had two things to talk about with Avellaneda, but we spent only one hour in the apartment and I spoke only of Jamie. She didn't say I was entirely blameless, and I thanked her for that. Mentally, of course. But I think, besides, that when a fellow becomes rotten there's no education can cure him, no attention that can straighten him out. Without doubt, I could have done more for him; that's so certain that I can't feel myself exempt from fault. But then what is it I really want? That he shouldn't be a homo, or simply to feel myself free of all blame? How selfish we are, my God, how selfish am I! Even to feel on good terms with one's conscience is a species of selfishness, of devotion to comfort, to the comfort of the spirit. . . . I didn't see Jaime.

FRIDAY, JULY 19

I didn't see him today, either. But I'm aware that Blanca has told him I want to talk with him. Esteban is a pretty violent boy. It would be better if he didn't know about his brother. Or perhaps he knows it already?

SATURDAY, JULY 20

Blanca brought me the envelope. The letter read like this: "Old man: I know you want to talk with me, and I know the theme beforehand. You are going to give me a moral preachment, and there are two reasons why I can't accept your sermon. The first is that I have nothing to reproach myself for. The second is that you yourself are living a secret life. I've seen you with the little dame who has snared you, and I think you'll agree with me that isn't the best way to keep the respect that's due to Mama's memory. But there you are with your one-sided puritanism. Since I don't like what you're doing, and you don't like what I'm doing, the best thing for me is to disappear. Hence—I disappear. You have a free field. I'm of age, don't worry about me. I also think that when I'm out of the way you'll get closer to my little siblings. Blanca knows all about it (for further information, apply to her). I told Esteban the story yesterday afternoon in his office. To make you feel better, I should confess that he reacted like a he man and gave me a black eye. The one I still have open allows me to see the future (it isn't so bad, you'll find) and to direct a final glance at my charming family, so beautiful and bourgeois. Salutations. Jaime." I passed the paper to Blanca. She took it slowly and said, "He's already taken his belongings. This morning." She was pale when she added, "The thing about the woman. Is that right?" "It is and it isn't," I said. "It's right that I have a connection with a woman—you might call her a girl. I live with her. It isn't true, on the other hand, that this means an offense to your mother. It seems to me that I have the right to love someone. Well, I love that girl. I haven't married her, only because I'm not sure that would be the most appropriate thing to do." Perhaps this last sentence was more than I should have said. I don't really know. She kept her lips tight closed. I think she was vacillating between a certain loyalty as a daughter and a very simple feeling of humanity. "But is she a good girl?" she asked seriously. "Yes, she's a good girl," I said. She gave a sigh of relief;

she still had confidence in me. I also sighed in relief, at the thought that I could provoke that confidence. Then I obeyed a sudden inspiration. "Is it too much to ask you to get to know her?" "I was going to ask you that myself," she said. I didn't make any remark, but the word of thanks was in my throat.

SUNDAY, JULY 21

"Perhaps, at the beginning, when Our Matter began, I would have preferred it. Now I think not." I note that down before anything else, for I'm afraid of forgetting it. That was her reply. For this time I spoke to her with complete frankness: the subject of marriage was discussed till it was exhausted. "Before we came here," she said, "to the apartment, I noticed that it was difficult for you to pronounce that word. One day you said it. It helped me to decide to believe in your affection. But I couldn't accept it, for it would have been a false basis for this present, which then was our future. To accept it, I should have had to accept also the idea that you would be giving way, that you would be obligating yourself to a decision for which you were not ripe. I gave way, on the other hand, because, as is logical, I could be surer of my reactions than of yours. I knew that even if I gave way I would not hold it against you; but if I forced you to give way I didn't know if that would leave you with some resentment against me. But now all that is over. Now I've 'fallen.' There's an ancient inheritance in a woman that makes her defend her virginity, to demand—and to impose on herself—the greatest guarantees to make up for her loss. Afterward, when she's 'fallen,' then she realizes that it was a myth, an old legend for capturing husbands. Hence at this moment I'm not sure that marriage is our best solution. The important thing is that we should be united by something; and that something does exist, isn't that so? Well, then, doesn't it seem to you more impressive, stronger, lovelier, that what unites us should be something that truly exists, and not a simple gesture, the ritual declaration made by an overworked, paunchy judge? Besides, there are your children. I don't want to look to you as if I were disputing your tie with the image of your Isabel, nor do I want them to feel jealous on behalf of their mother. And lastly there is your fear of what time may do, that you will grow old and I may start looking somewhere else. Don't be such a softie. What I like most about you is a quality that the passage of time won't be able to take away from you." These statements were more than her truths; they were my desires that she was expressing so calmly. And besides that, how agreeable they were to hear.

MONDAY, JULY 22

I made careful preparations for the meeting, but Avellaneda knew nothing in advance. We were in the pastry shop. We very seldom go out together. She is always nervous and thinks someone from the office is likely to see us. I tell her that sooner or later that's bound to happen. And I don't want us to spend our life locked in an apartment. Above her cup of chocolate she noticed my glance. "Whom did you see? Someone from there?" "There" is the office. "No, it's not from the office. But it's someone who wants to know you." She got so nervous that for a moment I was sorry I had brought on this confrontation. She followed the path of my look and recognized the other girl before I could say anything more. Blanca must have

[119]

some trait of mine. I called her with a gesture. I felt pretty proud of my fatherhood. "That's Blanca, my daughter." Avellaneda held out her hand. She was trembling. Blanca acted very well. "Please, don't be nervous. It was I who wanted to meet you." But Avellaneda didn't regain her equilibrium. She murmured, terribly ill at ease, "Heavens. I can't get used to the idea that he has spoken to you about me. I can't get used to the idea that you want to know me. Excuse me, I must look like I don't know what . . ." Blanca did everything possible to calm her; I too. In spite of the awkwardness, I could see that a bond of sympathy was being established between the two women. They are almost of the same age. In a short time Avellaneda became less disturbed; and after a bit her crying was over. In ten minutes they were conversing like two normal and civilized persons. I let them talk. It was a new pleasure to have both of them together with me, the two women I love most. When we separated (Avellaneda insisted with fervor that I should accompany my daughter), we walked a few blocks in the drizzle before taking the bus. Later, at home, Blanca gave me a hug, one of those hugs that she doesn't squander and which for that reason are the more memorable. With her cheek against mine she said, "I like her. I really do. I never believed you could make such a good choice." I ate very little, and went to bed. I'm as tired as though I had done a full year of hard labor. But that's nothing.

TUESDAY, JULY 23

I didn't see Avellaneda yesterday, after she left Blanca and me. Today, early, in the office, she came up to my desk with two large account books to consult me about something. We are always careful during work (until now no one has noticed anything). But today I looked at her closely. I wanted to know how she had come out of that trap I had laid for her. She was serious, very serious, almost without color in her cheeks. I gave her the instructions. We were surrounded by people, so we couldn't say anything to each other. But when she went away she took the opportunity to leave with me two stub books and a bit of paper with one scribbled word: "Thanks."

FRIDAY, JULY 26

8 A.M. I'm having breakfast at Tupi's. One of my greatest pleasures. To take a seat near any one of the windows that look out on the Plaza. It's raining. Still better. I've learned to love that folkloric monster called the Palacio Salvo. There's a reason why it figures in all the tourist posters. It's almost a representation of our national character: awkward, graceless, exaggerated, likable. It's ugly, so ugly that it puts one in good humor. I like Tupi's at that hour, very early, when the girlie-boys haven't yet invaded it (I had forgotten about Jaime, that nightmare), and there are only a few old men, each by himself, reading *El Día* or *El Debate* with extraordinary enjoyment. The majority are retired people who haven't been able to conquer the habit of getting up early. Does that mean that I'll be coming to Tupi's when I'm retired? Won't I be able to accustom myself to loll in bed until eleven o'clock, like some director's son? The true division of the social classes should be made on the basis of the hour when they get out of bed.

Biancamano comes up, the forgetful waiter, who gets by

with his simplicity and smiling face. For the fifth time I ask him for a demitasse with croissants, and he brings me a big cup with *traviatas*. His goodwill is so evident that I give up the fight. While I'm dropping the cubes of sugar in the cup he talks to me about the weather and his work. "This rain bothers people, but I say: Are we in winter or ain't we?" I tell him he's right, for it's evident that we are in winter. Then a gentleman calls him from a back table, pretty annoyed because Biancamano brought him something he hadn't ordered. He's one who won't give up. Or perhaps he's just an Argentinian, who came to make his weekly dollar deal and doesn't know the customs of the house. In the second part of my feast the newspapers arrive. There are days when I buy all of them. I like to recognize the features of each that never change. The style, full of syntactic gyrations, in the editorials of *El Debate;* the civilized understatement of *El País,* the informative jumble of *El Día,* interrupted here and there by another anticlerical effusion; the robust appearance of *La Mañana,* the only one that makes a profit. How different they are and how alike. Among them they play a kind of game, trying to fool each other, sending out signals, changing partners. But they all use the same deck of cards, they all feed on the same lies. And we read them, and on the basis of that reading we believe, we vote, we discuss. And we lose our memory; we forget generously, like morons, that they are saying today the opposite of what they said yesterday, that today they are defending with ardor the thing that yesterday they called a pestilence, and—worst of all—that today that same thing accepts the defense with satisfaction and pride. For that reason I prefer the candid frightfulness of the Palacio Salvo, for it has always been horrible, for it never fooled us, because it installed itself here, in the most frequented spot in the city, and for the past thirty years has obliged us all, natives or strangers, to raise our eyes in homage to its ugliness. To look at the newspapers you have to lower your eyes.

SATURDAY, JULY 27

She's enthusiastic over Blanca. "I never imagined you could have such an enchanting daughter." She said that to me every half hour, more or less. That phrase and Blanca's ("I never believed you could make such a good choice") aren't very complimentary to me; they didn't say much for the confidence they had placed in my capacity for choosing and of generating, respectively. But I'm satisfied. And Avellaneda too. Her scribbled "Thanks" of last Tuesday have since been amply developed. She confessed having passed a bad moment when she was brought face to face with my daughter. She thought that Blanca had come to make a scene, with all the reproaches that she imagined were in order, that she believed herself to deserve. She thought that the shock was going to be a violent one, so heavy, so destructive, that Our Matter wouldn't survive it. And only then did she fully realize how important Our Matter really was in her life, that perhaps it would now be impossible for her to do without a situation that until now she had considered clearly a provisional one. "You won't want to believe it, but all of that passed through my head while your daughter was coming up between the tables." Consequently, Blanca's friendly attitude came to her as an unexpected joy. "Tell me, could I be her friend?" is now her hopeful question, and she takes on a delicious expression, perhaps the same as she had twenty years ago when she asked her parents about Santa Claus.

There's no news of Jaime. Blanca asked at his office. He hasn't been there for ten days. Between Esteban and me there's a tacit agreement not to talk about the problem. It's been a blow for him too. I wonder how he'll react when he gets to know about Avellaneda's existence. I've asked Blanca not to tell him anything about it. For the present, at least. Perhaps I've carried things too far, by placing my children (or permitting them to place themselves) in the position of judges. I've done my duty by them. I've given them instruction, care, affection. Well, perhaps under the last heading I may have been a bit miserly. But it's because I can't be one of those types that are always going around with their hearts on their sleeves. It's hard for me to be affectionate, even in my love life. I always give less than I have. My style of loving is like that, a little reticent, reserving the maximum for the great occasions. Perhaps there's a reason for that; it's because I have a mania for nuances, for gradations. I figure that if I were always expressing the maximum, what would there be left for those moments (there are only four or five in every lifetime, in every individual) in which one should open one's heart to the full? Also I feel a certain revulsion before the ridiculous, and to me the ridiculous seems no more or less than to go around constantly with one's heart on one's sleeve. If someone cries every day, what remains for him to do when a real pain hits him, a pain that requires the maximum response? He can always kill himself, but that remains a poor solution in spite of everything. I mean that it is rather impossible to live in a permanent crisis, creating a sensibility that submerges one (as a kind of daily bath) in minor agonies. The good ladies say, with their customary feeling for psychological economics, that they won't go to the movies to see sad films because "life is bitter enough." And they are right in good part; life is bitter enough, without our having to make ourselves complainers or finicky or hysterical just because something has got in our way and doesn't let us pursue our excursion toward happiness, which at times is not very different from folly. I remember that one time, when the kids were going to school, there was an assignment in Jaime's class, one of those recurrent compositions on the classical theme of "mother." Jaime was nine years old, and he came home feeling very unhappy. I tried to make him understand that a thing like this was going to happen to him many times, that he had lost his mother, but he had to accept it; that it wasn't a thing to be crying about every day, and the best proof of affection that he could offer to the memory of his mother was just to show that her absence did not make him inferior to the others. Perhaps my language was inappropriate for his age. In any case, he stopped crying, looked at me with a hostility that made me shiver, and with the firmness of the inevitable, pronounced these words: "You are going to be my mother; if not, I'll kill you." What did he mean? He wasn't so small as not to know that he was demanding an absurd thing; but perhaps he wasn't big enough to hide his first suffering; the first of those daily agonies in which afterward he concentrated all his rancor, his rebelliousness, his frustration. The fact is that his teachers, his companions in society itself, demanded that he have a mother, and made him feel for the first time on that occasion the effect of her not being there. I don't know by what prodigy of imagination he attributed to me the sin of that absence. Perhaps he thought that if I had taken better care of her she would not have disappeared. I was the guilty one, therefore it was my duty to take her place. "If not, I'll kill you." He didn't kill me, of course, but he did succeed in killing himself, in annulling himself. Because the man of the family had failed him, he dedicated himself to denying the man he had within himself. Ugh! What an elaborate explanation for so simple, so ordinary, so unadornable a fact. My son is a fairy. A homo. One like that repellent Santini, the guy who has the sister who undresses. I would have preferred him to turn out a thief, a drug fiend, an imbecile. Perhaps I should feel pity for him, but I can't. I know there are understandable, perhaps valid, explanations for what he is. I know that many of these explanations would charge me with part of the fault. But why did Esteban and Blanca grow up normally, why didn't they go astray and the other one did? Precisely the other one, the one I loved the most. No, I won't feel pity. Not now, nor ever.

THURSDAY, AUGUST 1

The manager called me in. I could never stand him. He's an extremely common and cowardly type. Sometimes he has tried to reveal to me his soul, his abstract being, and what I got was an obnoxious image. Where normally one carries one's dignity he has nothing but a stump; it's been amputated. The prosthetic dignity that he uses now only gets him as far as smiling. Exactly; he was smiling when I came into his office. "Good news,

Santomé, good news." When he rubbed his hands continuously, I thought he was getting ready to hit me on the head. "They are offering you the assistant managership; imagine that!" I was sure that he had played no part in that offer from the board. "Allow me to congratulate you." He has a sticky hand, as if he had just opened a jar of jam. "Of course, on one condition." Now for "the stone behind the crab."

He really looked like a crab. Especially since at that moment he was walking sideways to get from behind his desk. "The condition is that you don't retire before two years." There go my dreams of leisure. It's a pretty job, being assistant manager, above all for finishing one's career in the enterprise. There isn't much to do; you take care of some important clients, you oversee the work of the force, you substitute for the manager when he is absent; your chief duty is to stand the directors and their horrible jokes, and the wives of the directors, with their exhibitions of encyclopedic ignorance. But my retirement? "How much time will I have to think it over?" I asked. It was an advance sign of my refusal. The eyes of the crab lit up and he said, "A week. I'll have to give your answer to the directors next Thursday." When I got back to my department, they all knew about it. That's the way it always happens with strictly confidential news. I was showered with hugs, congratulations, comments. Even the employee Avellaneda came up and shook hands with me.

SATURDAY, AUGUST 3

I had a long talk with her. She told me to think it over carefully, that the assistant managership is a comfortable, agreeable, respected job, well paid. OK. I know that too. But I know also that I have a right to rest, and that this right shouldn't be sold for one hundred more pesetas in salary. Perhaps I wouldn't sell it even if the offer were much higher. For me the essential thing has always been that what I earn should be enough for my needs. And what I have now is enough. I have a good salary. I don't need any more. Not even now with the extra expense of the apartment. When I retire, furthermore, I think I can count on a slightly higher income (almost one hundred pesos more), since the bonuses have raised my average earnings considerably over the past five years; and besides, I won't have any deductions. Still, I ought to consider the possible fall in the value of our money, which means, of course, that the cost of living will advance. The threat is certainly there, but I always have the possibility of carrying on some accounting work, more or less in secret. Of course, Avellaneda is making use, in addition, of some touching reasons, with less reference to filthy lucre: e.g., "If you're not there, the office will become unbearable." It's a better argument, but she doesn't convince me by that one, either, because I have a plan. When I retire, she'll stop working. What I'll have will be enough for the two of us. Besides, we're modest spenders. Our diversions, for obvious reasons, are strictly domestic. Sometimes we go to the movies, to a restaurant, to a pastry place. On Sundays sometimes, when it's cold but the sun is shining, we walk on the beach, to breathe better. We buy a book or two, a record or two; but more than anything else we are entertained by talking, talking about ourselves, by going back to that period of our lives which antedated Our Matter. There's no theater or diversion of any sort that can take the place of what we enjoy in this exercise of sincerity and complete frankness. We're now getting quite skillful at it. But we still have to get accustomed to being sincere. During all those years in which Aníbal was out of the country; with so many problems of communication in my relations with my children; with my defensive reticence that always protected my life from malicious comment at the office; with my contacts, merely hygienic, with constantly changing women, it's evident that I had grown out of the habit of being sincere. It's even probable that only in a sporadic form had I been practicing it with myself. I say that because sometimes, in these frank conversations with Avellaneda, I have found myself saying words that seem to me to be more sincere even than my thoughts. Could that be possible?

SUNDAY, AUGUST 4

This morning I opened a drawer of my little dresser, and an unexpected quantity of photos, clippings, letters, receipts and memos fell to the floor. Then I saw a paper of indefinite color (it's probable that it was originally green, but now it has some dark stains, made by the ink that ran due to ancient moistures, now dried up forever). Until that moment I had absolutely no recollection of its existence, but as soon as I saw it I recognized Isabel's letter. We didn't write many letters, Isabel and I. (We really had no reason to do so, since there were no long separations.) The letter was dated at Tacuarembó, October 17, 1935. I felt rather strange in front of those slender characters, with long, carefully formed tails, in which it was possible to recognize a person and even an epoch. Evidently it hadn't been written by a fountain pen, but by one of those spoon-shaped nibs that, as soon as you forced them to write, started to make complaining noises and even scatter tiny drops of almost invisible violet ink all about them. I'll have to transcribe the letter in this notebook. I must do it because it is part of myself, of my ineradicable history. It was sent to me under very special circumstances, and rereading it has thrown me off base a little.

Here it is: "My Beloved, it's three weeks since I arrived here. Translation: three weeks that I've been sleeping alone. Doesn't that seem horrible to you? You know that at times I wake up at night and find it absolutely necessary to touch you, to feel you at my side. I don't know what you have that comforts me, but knowing that you are near makes me feel under your protection even when I'm half asleep. Now I have terrible nightmares, but my nightmares don't have monsters. They just consist of dreaming that I'm alone in the bed, without you. And when I wake up, and the nightmare flees away, it turns out that in fact I am alone in bed, without you. The only difference is that in my dream I can't cry, and, contrariwise, when I awake I do cry. Why does that happen to me? I know that you are there in Montevideo; I know that you are taking care of yourself, I know you think about me. That's so, isn't it? Esteban and the little girl are well, although you know that Aunt Zulma spoils them too much. Prepare yourself for the fact that, when we come back, the little girl won't let us sleep for a few nights. God, when will those few nights come?

"I have news for you; can you guess? Yes, I'm that way again. It's horrible to be telling you that, and you not kissing me. Or perhaps that isn't so horrible for you? It'll be a boy, and we'll call him Jaime. I like names that begin with J. I don't know why, but this time I'm a little afraid. And if I should die? Answer me right away telling me no, I'm not going to die. Have you ever thought what you would do if I were to die? You're a strong sort, you can take care of yourself; besides, you'll meet another woman right away, and I'm fearfully jealous already of her. Do you see how neurasthenic I am? It's because it hurts me a lot not to have you here, or that you don't have me there—it's the same thing. Don't laugh; you're always laughing at everything, even if there's nothing funny about it. Don't laugh, don't be bad. Write me and tell me I'm not going to die. Not even as a soul in pain could I stop scolding you when you laugh like that.

"Ah, before I forget it: I spoke on the phone to Maruja to remind her that the 22nd is Dora's birthday. To congratulate her for herself and me. Is the house filthy? Did the girl come to clean it—the one Celia recommended to me? Take care not to look at her too much, eh? Aunt Zulma is happy to have the children here. To say nothing about Uncle Eduardo. They tell me all sorts of stories about you, about when you were ten years old and used to come here to spend your vacations. It seems you made yourself famous by your answers to everything. Quite a boy, says Uncle Eduardo. I think you're still quite a boy, even when you come home from the office all tired out, and there's a trace of resentment in your eyes, and you treat me with indifference, sometimes with hostility. But we're all right at night, isn't that so? It's been raining for the past three days. I sit by the balcony of the living room and look out on the street. But not a soul passes on the street. When the kids are asleep I go to Uncle Eduardo's study and entertain myself with the Spanish-English Dictionary. My culture and my boredom are both growing at a great rate. Will it be a boy or a girl? If it's a girl you can choose her name, provided always it isn't Leonor. But no. It's got to be a boy and his name will be Jaime; and he'll have a long face like yours and will be very ugly and have lots of success with women. Look, I like children, I love them very much, but what I like most is that they are your children. Now it's raining furiously on the paving stones. I'm going to do the five-pile solitaire, the one that Dora taught me. Remember? If I succeed, that'll mean I won't die in childbirth. I love you, I love you, I love you, Your Isabel. P.S. The solitaire came out right! Hurrah!"

From a distance of twenty-two years, how vulnerable that enthusiasm seems. However, it was legitimate, honest, based on certainty. It's strange that in reading that letter I've been able once again to see Isabel's face, that face which, in spite of my forgettings, was still in my memory. And I found it in those *tu*'s, those *puedes*'s, those *tienes*'s. For Isabel never used the *vos* to me, and not from any conviction, but merely by habit, or perhaps from some quirk. I read those *tu*'s and right away I could reconstruct the mouth that said them. And for Isabel her mouth was the most important part of her face. The letter is like *she* was: a little chaotic, a perpetual movement from optimism to pessimism and vice versa, always turning about our love in bed, full of apprehensions, mobile. Poor Isabel. The child was male and was called Jaime; but she died from an attack of eclampsia, a few hours after giving birth. Jaime doesn't have a long face like mine. He's not at all ugly, and his success with women is only superficial and quite useless to boot. Poor Isabel. She believed that in succeeding in her game of solitaire she had brought destiny over to her side, but she had only given it a provocation. It's all so far away, so far away. Even including Isabel's husband, to whom the letter of 1935 was addressed and who was myself, even he is so far removed, I don't know whether for good or for bad. "Don't laugh," she told me, and repeated it. And it was true: I did laugh a lot at that time, and my laughter made a bad impression on her. She didn't like the wrinkles that formed next to my eyes when I laughed, nor did she find the cause of my laughter funny; she couldn't help turning aggressive and troublesome when I laughed. When we were with other people and I laughed she looked at me with censuring eyes, which gave advance notice of the reproach to come when we were alone. "Don't laugh, please. It makes you look horrible." When she died, the laughter left my mouth. I went around for about a year bowed down by three things: grief, work and the children. Afterward my equilibrium returned, my aplomb, my calm. But laughter didn't return. Well, I do laugh at times, of course, but for some special reason and because I consciously want to laugh. On the other hand, that laugh that was almost a tic, a permanent gesture, it didn't come back. At times I think it's too bad that Isabel isn't here to see me so serious; she would have got much satisfaction out of my present solemnity. But perhaps, if Isabel were here, with me, she would not have cured me of laughing. Poor Isabel. Now I realize that I talked with her very little. At times we had nothing to talk about; we didn't really have many common themes between us, apart from the children, the bills and sex. But we really didn't need to talk about this last theme. Was that love? I'm not sure. It's likely that if our marriage hadn't ended after five years, we would have noticed later that sex was only one of its ingredients. Perhaps not much later. But during those five years it was the ingredient that succeeded in keeping us united, strongly united. Now, with Avellaneda, sex is (for me, at least) a less important, less vital ingredient; much more important and vital are our conversations, our affinities. But I mustn't get overenthusiastic. I'm well aware that now I'm forty-nine years old, and when Isabel died I was twenty-seven. It's more than certain that if Isabel appeared now, the same Isabel of 1935 who wrote that letter from Tacuarembó, an Isabel with black hair, come-on eyes, touchable hips, perfect legs, it's more than certain that I would say, "Isn't it too bad," and go off to look for Avellaneda.

WEDNESDAY, AUGUST 7

There's another thing to bear in mind in considering the opportunity of being assistant manager. If Avellaneda had not come into my life, perhaps I'd have the right to hesitate before turning it down. I understand that for some people leisure can be fatal; I know of various retired people who weren't able to survive the interruption of their routine. But these are the people who had grown all stiff and creaky inside, with ankylosed spirits, as it were, who had virtually ceased to think for themselves. I don't believe that would happen to me. I think for myself. But even thinking for myself I could mistrust leisure as long as it would be a simple form of solitude; as it had the possibility of being a few months ago, before Avellaneda appeared. But with her installed in my existence, now there won't be any solitude. That is to say, I hope to God there won't be. A man has to be more modest when he confronts himself, when he confides in himself, when he gets close to his final truth, which could still become more decisive than the voice of conscience—for the latter suffers from inability to speak, from unexpected attacks of hoarseness that now and then prevent it from being audible. I know now that my loneliness was a horrible phantom. I know that the mere presence of Avellaneda has been enough to scare it away; but I know also that it isn't dead, that it will be gathering its forces in some unclean underground section of my routine. For that reason I climb down from my self-sufficiency and constrain myself to say, "I hope to God . . ."

THURSDAY, AUGUST 8

What a relief. I answered no. The manager smiled with satisfaction, first because he wouldn't like me for a collaborator, and also because my negative answer will help him validate the good reasons which he surely had advanced to oppose my promotion. "That's what I said: a man that's finished, a man that doesn't want to struggle. For this job we need an active, enterprising type, not a fellow that's worn out." I can see the play of his loathsome thumb, moving coarsely, boastfully, egocentrically. Business concluded. What tranquillity.

MONDAY, AUGUST 12

Yesterday afternoon we were seated together at the table. We weren't doing anything, not even talking. I was resting my hand on an ashtray with no ashes. We were sad; that's the way we were—sad. But it was a sweet sadness, almost a sense of peace. She was looking at me, and all at once she moved her lips to say three words. She said, "I love you." Then I realized that it was the first time she had said that to me; even more, it was the first time she had said that to anyone. Isabel had repeated that to me twenty times a night. For Isabel, to repeat that was like giving another kiss; it was a simple part of the love game. Avellaneda, by contrast, had said it once, when it was needed. Perhaps now she won't have to say it again, because it isn't a game; it's an essence. Then I felt a tremendous pressure on my chest, but it was an oppression in which no physical organ seemed to be affected; nevertheless, it was almost asphyxiating, unbearable. There in my breast, near my throat, I felt a lump. "Until now I didn't say that to you," she murmured, "not because I didn't love you but because I didn't know why I loved you. But now I know." I could breathe then; it seemed to me that the little burst of air came from the depth of my stomach. I can always breathe better when someone explains things. The delight before a mystery, the enjoyment in face of the unexpected, are sensations that at times my modest forces are unable to support. She always explains things better than anyone else. . . . "Now I know. I don't love you for your face, or for your age, or for your words, or for your intentions. I love you because you're made of good stuff." No one ever had favored me with a judgment so simple, so moving, so life-giving. I want to think that's right, I want to believe that I'm made of good stuff. Perhaps that moment was a very exceptional one, but anyhow I felt I was alive. That oppression in the bosom means being alive.

Next Monday I'll start my last vacation. It will be an anticipation of the great Final Leisure. Jaime has given no signs of life.

FRIDAY, AUGUST **16**

A really embarrassing incident. I had met Aníbal at six-thirty, and after chatting for a while in the café, we took the trolley. It was convenient for him too, since he gets off before me. We talked about women, marriage, fidelity, etc. All in very sweeping and general terms. I spoke in a low voice, because I've always been wary of people's ears when traveling, but Aníbal, even when he wants to impart a secret, does so in a stentorian shout that inundates the air around. I don't know to what concrete case we were referring. Standing next to him, in the vestibule, I saw an old woman with a square face and a round hat. I noticed that she was hanging on Aníbal's words, but since what he was saying was very edifying, very petit-bourgeois, and moral as can be, I wasn't too worried. However, when Aníbal got off and the old woman came over to take a seat next to me, the first thing she said was, "Don't pay any attention to that diabolical person." And before I could give utterance to an astonished "What do you mean?" the old lady was already continuing with, "A truly diabolical type. It's that kind that bring homes to ruin. Oh, you men! How easily you condemn women! Look, I can assure you that whenever a woman falls, there is always a destructive, stupid, demoralizing man who first made her lose faith in herself." The old woman was talking at the top of her voice. All the heads began to turn to see who was the recipient of that kind of lecture. And I felt like a worm. She went on. "I'm a follower of Batlle, but I'm against divorce. Divorce is what has killed the family. Do you know where that devilish adviser of yours is going to end? Oh, you don't know, but I do. He'll either end in jail or he'll commit suicide, and it would be good if he did it. For I know men that we ought to burn alive." I pictured to myself the unlikely image of Aníbal being toasted in a flaming pyre. It was only then that I found breath to respond. "Tell me, lady, why don't you shut up? What do you know of the problem? What the gentleman has just said was precisely the opposite of what you understood." And the old woman, paying no attention: "Think of the old-time families. There, people were moral. You would pass in late afternoon by those homes and you'd see, seated on the veranda, the husband, the wife, the children—all with good sense, dignified, well-educated. That is happiness, sir, and it's not a question of whether the woman is ruined, whether she takes up a life of shame. For at bottom, no woman is really bad, understand?" And while she was yelling that at me, waving her forefinger, her hat had got displaced somewhat to the left. I must say that her image of the whole family seated on the veranda didn't succeed in moving me too much. "You don't take me seriously, mister. You just laugh, that's all you know how to do." "And why don't you laugh yourself, instead of getting all hot and bothered?" The people had begun to make remarks. The old woman had her partisans, and I had mine. When I say "I," I mean that hypothetical and phantom enemy against whom the lady was discharging her insults. "And take into account that I am a follower of Batlle, but opposed to divorce." Then, before she could start the ominous cycle over again, I excused myself and got off the trolley ten blocks from my destination.

SATURDAY, AUGUST 17

This morning I was talking with two members of the board. The subjects were of no great importance, but they succeeded in making me understand that what they felt for me was a friendly but comprehensive contempt. I imagine that, when they ensconce themselves in the soft-cushioned armchairs of the Directors' Room, they must feel omnipotent—at least as close to Olympus as an unclean and sinful soul can feel. They have reached the high point. For a football player the high point means getting to be a member of the national team; for a mystic, to communicate with God; for a person of feeling, to find on some occasion in another being the true echo of his own sentiments. But for this poor tribe, by contrast, the high spot is being able to sit in the great directorial armchairs, and to experience the sensation (for others it would be mighty uncomfortable) of holding certain destinies in their hands; to give themselves the illusion that they are resolvers, that they are disposers, that they are Somebodies. Today, when I regarded them, I didn't find in each the face of a Somebody, but rather of a Something. They seemed to me to be Things, not Persons. But how would I appear to them? Once, many years ago, I heard the oldest of them say, "The great mistake of some businessmen is to treat their employees as if they were human." I never forgot and never shall forget that sentence, because I can't excuse it. Not only in my name but in the name of the whole human race. Now I feel a great temptation to turn the sentence around, and to think: "The great mistake of some employees is to treat their bosses as if they were persons." But I must resist that temptation. They *are* persons. And persons worthy of a hateful pity, of the most infamous of all pities, because the truth is that they adopt a shell of arrogance, a repellent air of importance, a hypocritical solidity, but at bottom they are hollow. And they are suffering from the most horrible variation of loneliness: the loneliness of the man who can't even stand himself.

SUNDAY, AUGUST 18

"Tell me about Isabel." Avellaneda has this good trait: she makes one discover things about oneself, makes one know oneself better. When people remain alone for a long time, when many years pass without that life-giving and searching dialogue which stimulates us to advance from mere lucidity to the more intricate zones of instinct, toward those really virgin, unexplored regions of the desires, the feelings, the repulsions—when this solitude is converted into a routine, then we lose the capacity to react to impulses, to feel alive. That was happening to me. But now Avellaneda comes and asks questions, and from the questions she puts I ask myself many more, and thus it comes about—now—that I feel jolted into life. "Tell me about Isabel" is an innocent and simple question, but nonetheless . . . What pertained to Isabel pertains to me, or did; they were the kinds of things that I was in Isabel's time. God, how immature I was! When Isabel came on the scene I didn't know what I wanted, I didn't know what to expect from her or from myself. I didn't have standards of comparison then; I had no patterns by which even to recognize when I was happy and when unhappy. It was our good moments that later formed my definition of happiness, and our bad moments served to create the formula for unhappiness. One might also call that freshness, spontaneity; but how many abysses are contained in spontaneity! Yet I was lucky in the midst of it all. Isabel was a good sort; and I wasn't an idiot. Our union was never a complicated thing. But what would have happened if time had succeeded in spoiling that vulnerable charm of sex? "Tell me things about Isabel" is an invitation to sincerity. I knew the risk I was running. Jealousies of past events (because they do not admit of a true grudge, because they are based on no real challenge, because they deal with a phantom rivalry) are frightfully cruel. Nevertheless, I was sincere. I told things about Isabel that really belonged to her. And to me. I didn't invent an Isabel that would allow me to show off before Avellaneda. Of course, I had the impulse to do that. We always like to look good, and we want to look better than good before the person we love, in whose eyes we want to acquire merit in order to be loved in our turn. I didn't invent, first because I believe that Avellaneda is worthy of the truth; and then, also, because I too am worthy, because I am tired (and in this case my fatigue is almost a disgust) of making believe, of this make-believe that one places like a mask over one's old and too sensitive countenance. Hence I wasn't surprised by the fact that, while Avellaneda was learning how Isabel had been, I too was getting to know how I myself had been.

MONDAY, AUGUST 19

Today I began my last vacation. It rained all day. I spent the whole afternoon in the apartment. I changed three electric outlets, painted a wardrobe and washed my nylon shirts. At 6:30 Avellaneda arrived, but she stayed only until 8 P.M. She had to go to a birthday celebration for an aunt. She said that Muñoz, as my substitute, is insufferably bossy and pedantic. There's already been an incident with Robledo.

TUESDAY, AUGUST 20

It's a month now since Jaime left the house. Whether I think about it or not, there's no denying that the problem is always with me. If only I had been able to talk just once with him!

WEDNESDAY, AUGUST 21

I stayed at home and read I don't know how many hours. I don't want to do any more than that. I am seized by a horrible sensation of time being wasted, somewhat as if stupidity were anesthetizing my brain.

THURSDAY, AUGUST 22

I feel a little strange without the office. But perhaps I feel that way because I am conscious that this is not real leisure, it's only a leisure with an expiration date, it's still threatened by the office.

I wanted to give her a surprise. I stationed myself a block away from the office. At six-thirty I saw her coming near. But she was coming with Robledo. It's a fact that she was laughing unrestrainedly, really amused. Since when has Robledo become so witty? I got into a café, let them pass, and then began to walk about thirty steps behind them. When they got to Andes Street, they parted. She turned around toward San José Street. She was going to the apartment, of course. I went into a rather dirty café, where they served me a cup that still had lipstick on it. I didn't drink it, but I didn't ask the waiter for another, either. I was agitated, nervous, unsettled. Above all I was angry at myself. Avellaneda laughing with Robledo. What was wrong with that? Avellaneda in a simple human relationship, not merely at the office, with a chap other than me. Avellaneda, walking in the street next to a young man, one of her generation, not a has-been like me. Avellaneda far away from me. Avellaneda laughing without thinking about me. Avellaneda living on her own. Of course there was nothing wrong about all that. But perhaps the horrible sensation came from the fact that this was the first time that I was completely aware of the possibility that Avellaneda can exist and function and laugh without having need of my protection (let's not say of my love). I knew that the conversation between her and Robledo had been an innocent one. Or perhaps not. For Robledo has no way of knowing that she isn't free. How idiotic, how cheap, how conventional I seem to myself in writing "She isn't free." Free for what? Perhaps the essence of my disquietude lies merely in my discovery that she can feel very much at ease with young people, especially with a young man. And besides, what I saw wasn't anything; but, against that, what I half glimpsed was a lot—what I half glimpsed was the risk of losing everything. Robledo is not important. At bottom he's a frivolous fellow who could never succeed in interesting her. Except that I don't know her absolutely. Well, shall I ever know her? Robledo is not the question. But the others, all the others in the world? If one young man makes her laugh, how many others could make her fall in love? If she should lose me someday (her only danger of that happening is through death, which has us all on file), she would still have her heart, which will always be new, generous, splendid. But if I should lose her one day (my only danger of that is through man, the man who stands in every corner of the world, the man who is young and who makes promises), I would lose with her my last opportunity to really live, my last participation in time; for just as now my heart feels itself generous, lively, renewed, without her it would once again become forlorn and decrepit.

I paid for the beverage I hadn't drunk and proceeded to the apartment. I was afraid, and ashamed of my fear, that she might say nothing about it, above all because I knew in advance that even if she were silent I would not do any investigating or cross-examining or reproaching. I was simply going to swallow my bitterness, and so begin an era of little torments without surcease. I hold a particular mistrust of my gray periods. I believe my hand trembled when I turned the key in the lock. "How come you're arriving so late?" she called from the kitchen. "I was waiting for you, to tell you the last crazy thing of Robledo—what a character! I haven't laughed so much for years." And she appeared in the living room with her apron, her green skirt, her black blouse, her eyes limpid, warm, sincere. She could have no idea how she was saving my life by those words. I drew her toward me, and while I embraced her, while I breathed in the soft, animal odor of her shoulders through the other, very special odor of the wool, I felt that the world was starting to turn again, I felt I could relegate once more to a distant and unnamed future that concrete menace that I had called "Avellaneda and the others." "Avellaneda and I," I said quietly. She didn't understand the reason for these three words on that precise occasion, but some obscure instinct told her that something important had happened. She pulled away a little from me, but without letting me go, and demanded, "Let's see now; say that again." "Avellaneda and I," I repeated, obediently. . . . Now I'm alone, having returned home, and it's almost two in the morning. From time to time, merely because it gives me strength and firmness and inner harmony, I repeat over and over: "Avellaneda and I."

SATURDAY, AUGUST 24

It's only rarely that I think about God. However, I do have a religious base, an anxiety about religion. I want to convince myself that I really possess a definition, a conception of God. But I don't possess anything of the kind. I don't often think about God, simply because the problem is so elevated, so completely above me that it provokes a kind of panic inside me, a general dissipation of my power to think clearly and to reason logically. "God is the Totality," Avellaneda often says. "God is the Essence of everything," says Aníbal. "He is what maintains it all in harmony; God is the great Coherence." I can understand both of these definitions, but neither of them is my definition. It's probable that the other two are quite satisfied with theirs, but that's not the God I need. I need a God I can have a dialogue with, a God in whom I can seek support, a God who answers me when I question him, when I shower him with my doubts. If God is the Totality, the great Coherence, if God is only the energy that keeps the universe alive, if he is something so immeasurably infinite, what importance to him can I have, who am only an atom badly attached to an insignificant louse of his Kingdom? I'm not worried about being an atom of the littlest louse of his Kingdom, but I am concerned that God should be within my reach; I must be able to seize him, not with my hands, of course, not even with my reason. It is most important for me to take hold of him with my heart.

SUNDAY, AUGUST 25

She brought me photos of her childhood, her family, her world. That's a proof of love, isn't it? She was a slender little creature with somewhat frightened eyes and straight black hair. An only daughter. I too was an only child. That's not an easy thing to be. You finish by feeling abandoned. There's a delicious photograph in which she appears with an enormous police dog, and the animal is gazing at her with a protective air. I imagine to myself that the whole world would have always wanted to protect her. However, she doesn't feel so helpless; she's quite sure of what she wants. Besides, I like her being sure about things. She's sure that work suffocates her, that she'll never commit suicide, that Marxism is a great error, that she likes me, that death is not the end of everything, that her parents are magnificent, that God exists, that the people she has faith in will never fail her. I could never be that categorical. But the best of all is that she's right. Her sureness serves even to frighten Fate. There's a picture of her with her parents, when she was twelve. Starting with this likeness, I too went to work to construct my impression of that singular, harmonious, unusual marriage. The mother is a woman of soft traits, fine nose, black hair, very light skin, with two dimples in her left cheek. Her eyes are tranquil, perhaps too much so; perhaps they don't engage themselves completely in the spectacle of which they're a part, and in which they've come to live; but they appear to me capable of understanding everything. He is a tall man, with rather narrow shoulders, on whom baldness has already made some ravages; he has very thin lips and a sharp but not aggressive chin. I pay a lot of attention to people's eyes. His have something strange about them. Not of alienation in the medical sense, but rather of philosophical alienation. They are the eyes of a fellow who is surprised by the world, by the mere fact of finding himself in it. They are both good people (that's visible in their faces), but I prefer her goodness to his. The father is an excellent man, but he's not capable of communicating with the world. Indeed, one can't know what would happen if and when he succeeded in establishing that communication. "They love each other," said Avellaneda, "but I don't know if that is the kind of love that I like." She shook her head to accompany the expression of doubt, then she added with animation, "In the range of sentiments there is a series of neighboring zones, which are similar and easy to confound. Love, confidence, pity, comradeship, tenderness—I don't know in which of those zones the relations of Mother and Father have their place. It's something very difficult to define, and I don't believe that they themselves have defined it. Now and then I've spoken on this subject with Mother. She thinks there's too much serenity in her union with Father, too much equilibrium to allow the full existence of love. This serenity, this equilibrium, these things that could also be called lack of passion, might perhaps have been intolerable if my parents had had anything to reproach one another for. But there are no reproaches or reasons for reproach. They know that both of them are good, honest, generous. They know besides that these things, magnificent as they are, still don't mean love, don't signify that they are burning in that fire. They're not burning, but that which unites them lasts all the longer." "And what is happening with you and me? Are we burning?" I asked. But in that precise instant something distracted her, and her look too seemed like that of a person surprised by the world, by the mere fact of finding herself in it.

MONDAY, AUGUST 26

I told Esteban about Avellaneda. Blanca had gone to lunch with Diego, so we were alone at noontime. It was a great relief to learn that he already knew. Jaime had given him the information. "Look, Papá, I can't understand it completely, nor do I believe that it's the best solution for you to have taken up with a girl so much younger than you. But one thing is certain: I wouldn't dare to judge you. I know that when one views things from the outside, when one doesn't feel himself involved in them, it's very easy to declare what is wrong and what is right. When you're plunged up to the neck in a problem (and I've been in that position many times), then things change, there is a different intensity, deep convictions appear that demand sacrifices and renunciations that could seem inexplicable to a mere observer. My greatest wish is that it will turn out well, not superficially well, but truly well. I want you to feel at the same time protector and protected, and that is one of the most agreeable sensations any human being could have. I remember very little of Mother. I do have some sort of a true picture, but on it have been superimposed images and memories coming from other people. And I don't know which of these memories are exclusively mine. Perhaps only this one: of her combing her hair in the bedroom, with her long, dark hair falling on her shoulder. So you see that there isn't much that I remember of Mother. But with the years I've been accustoming myself to consider her as something ideal, unattainable, almost ethereal. She was so pretty. Isn't that so? I realize that at best my representation of her has little relation with what Mother truly was. However, it's that way that she exists for me. So I was rather shocked when Jaime told me that you were going with a girl. It shocked me, but I accept it, for I know that you are very much alone. And I realize it the more now, because I've been watching this new development and I've seen you come back to life. Consequently, I'm not judging you; I couldn't judge you. Most of all, I'd be very glad if you were getting as close as possible to true happiness."

TUESDAY, AUGUST 27

Cold and sun. The winter sun, which is the most affectionate, the most benevolent. I went up to Plaza Matriz and sat down on a bench, after opening up a newspaper to protect me from the pigeons' attentions. In front of me a municipal worker cleaned the greensward. He did it most sparingly, as if he were above all enthusiasm. How would I feel if I were a municipal employee cleaning up the lawn? No, that's not my vocation. If I could choose a profession different from the one I have, another routine from that which has been wearing me out for the past thirty years, I'd choose to be a waiter in a café. I'd be an active, unforgetful, exemplary waiter. I'd try to find mental tricks, so as not to lose count of anybody's orders. It would be wonderful to work all the time with new faces, to speak freely with a chap who comes in today, orders coffee and never comes back again. People as a whole are formidable, interesting, capable of anything. It must be fabulous to work with people instead of working with numbers, books, files. Even though I should travel far from here, where I could be impressed by landscapes, monuments, roads, works of art, nothing could fascinate me as much as people—just to see people passing and to scrutinize their faces, to recognize here and there gestures of happiness and of bitterness, to see how they dash toward their destinies, in an insatiable turbulence, in a splendid rush, and to realize how they are pushing on, unconscious of their own brevity, their insignificance, their life with no reserves to fall back on, and without ever feeling corralled, without admitting that they are imprisoned. I believe that up to now I had never been conscious of the existence of Plaza Matriz. I must have crossed it a thousand times; perhaps for the same number of times I swore at the detour we must make to pass around the fountain. I've seen it before, of course, but I never stopped to observe it, to feel it, to extract and recognize its character. I spent a goodly time contemplating the aggressively solid *alma* of the Cabildo, the hypocritically washed countenance of the cathedral, the breathless nodding of the trees. I think that in that moment I reached a definite conviction: I belong to this place, to this city. In that one thing (and probably in nothing else) I believe I must be a fatalist. Everyone is of a certain spot on earth, and there he has to pay his due. I am of this place. It's here that I pay my quota. That man who is passing (he of the long overcoat, the projecting ears, the angry limp)—that man is like me. He still doesn't know that I exist, but one day he will see me full face, or in profile, or from the back, and he'll have the sensation that between us there is some secret, a hidden bond that unites us, that gives us the power to understand each other. Or perhaps that day will never arrive; perhaps he'll never pay attention to this plaza, to this air which makes us neighbors, which couples us, which connects us. But that doesn't matter; in any case he and I are alike.

WEDNESDAY, AUGUST 28

I've got only four days of vacation left. I don't miss the office. I miss Avellaneda. Today I went to the cinema, alone. I saw a Western. Up to the middle I found it entertaining; but after that I got bored with myself, with my own patience.

THURSDAY, AUGUST 29

I asked Avellaneda to stay away from the office. I, her boss, gave her permission, and that sufficed. She spent the whole day with me in the apartment. I can imagine the rumpus made by Muñoz, with two people less in the section, and all the responsibility on his shoulders. I not only imagine it but I sympathize with it. But what of it? I'm of an age at which time seems and really is irretrievable. I have to lay hold desperately of this sensible happiness which has searched me out. For that reason I can't become magnanimous and generous. I can't start thinking about the troubles of Muñoz before my own. My life is passing, it's on its way right now, and I can't endure that feeling of something escaping, finishing and over with. This day with Avellaneda isn't eternity; it's just one day, a poor, unworthy, limited day, which all of us, from God down, have condemned to perish. It is not eternity, but it is the instant, which, after all, is eternity's only true substitute. Consequently I must seize it in my fist, and then spend it all, without any reserve or foresight. Perhaps later on I'll have many days like this one, and then I'll think about this worry, this impatience, as a ridiculous drain of energy. Perhaps, only perhaps. But this meanwhile holds the comfort, the guarantee of that which is, of that which is going on now.

It was cold. Avellaneda spent the whole day in a turtleneck sweater and trousers. That way, and with her hair done up, she looked like a boy. I told her she had the face of a newsboy. But she didn't pay much attention to me. She was preoccupied with her horoscope. A year ago someone cast her horoscope and predicted her future. It seems that in that future there figured her present job and, above all, I figured too. "A mature man, of great goodness, not very distinguished, but intelligent." Hello! That's me. She: "What do you think? Can one predict the future?" I: "I don't know if it can be done, but in any case it seems to me a fraud. I don't want to know what's going to happen to me. That would be horrible. Can you imagine how frightful life would be if one knew when one was going to die?" She: "As for me, I'd like to know when I'm going to die. If we could know the date of our death, we could regulate the rhythm of our life, and spend more or spend less in accordance with the balance that will remain." That seemed monstrous to me. But the prediction said that Avellaneda will have two or three children, that she will be happy but will be left a widow (bah), that she will die of a circulatory ailment, sometime in her eighties. Avellaneda was much concerned about those two or three children. She: "Do you want to have them?" I: "I'm not too sure." She realized that my reply was the essence of prudence; but when she looks at me I know that she would like to have children— one, at any rate. "Don't be sad," I said. "If you get sad, I'm capable of giving you twins." She knows what I'm thinking, suffers on that account, but she clings to the prophecy. "And aren't you concerned about being a widow, even though it be a clandestine widowhood?" "I'm not concerned about that, because my faith in the forecast doesn't go that far. I know that you are indestructible, that all predictions pass you by, without touching you." She was nothing but a child who had climbed on the sofa, with her legs doubled up, and the point of her nose red with cold.

FRIDAY, AUGUST **30**

During my vacation I wrote her every day. It will be an uphill job getting back into the work routine. This time out has been a good preliminary for my retirement. Blanca received a letter from Jaime today; it was full of rancor and violence. The paragraph he dedicated to me runs like this: "Tell the old man that all my love affairs were platonic, so that, when he has nightmares over what appears to be my unclean person, he can turn over and breathe tranquilly. For now." There's too much hatred joined together in that for it to be true. In the end I'm going to believe that my son loves me a little.

SATURDAY, AUGUST 31

Avellaneda and Blanca have been seeing each other without my knowing it. Blanca let fall a revealing little sentence, and all was in the open. "We didn't want to tell you about it, because we were learning a lot about you." At first I thought of that as a bad joke, but afterward I was touched. I couldn't do any more than imagine to myself the two girls exchanging their respective incomplete images of the simple type that is me. A kind of jigsaw puzzle. There's curiosity in that, of course, but also there's affection. Avellaneda, for her part, showed herself very apologetic, asked my pardon and said for the hundredth time that Blanca was stupendous. I'm glad they're friends, for my sake, through me, because of me, but I can't escape the sensation at times of being de trop. In reality, I'm an old man with whom two children are occupying themselves.

SUNDAY, SEPTEMBER 1

The spree is over. Tomorrow back to the office. I think of the sales lists, the large eraser, the books of carbon copies, the check stubs, the manager's voice—and my stomach turns.

They received me as a savior, with all the problems still to be solved. It appears that an inspector had been there and made a terrible fuss about some silly thing. Muñoz, poor guy, loses his head at the least difficulty. I found Santini more of a fairy than usual. He made some pretty scandalous advances to me. Would that also be platonic? They say that, since I refuse the job, they'll bring in an assistant manager from the outside. Martínez is the one who's sore as hell. Today, for the first time since the blowup, I saw the Valverde girl. She moves her behind with an enthusiasm worthy of a better cause.

For the first time Avellaneda spoke to me about her former fiancé. His name is Enrique Avalos and he works for the city. The engagement lasted only one year. Exactly—from April a year ago until this April. "He's a good sort. I still think well of him, but . . ." I realize that I've always been afraid of that explanation, but also that my greatest fear was that I'd never hear it. Since she dared to mention it now, it must be because the subject is no longer of such importance. In any case all my senses were hanging on that "but," which sounded to me like celestial music. Because the fiancé had possessed all the advantages (his age, his appearance, the mere fact of being there first) and perhaps he hadn't known how to profit from them. Starting with that "but" my advantages began, and I surely was disposed to profit from them, that is to say, to undermine poor Enrico Avalos's position. Experience has taught me that one of the best ways of defeating a rival in the vacillating heart of a woman is to praise this same rival unrestrictedly, to show yourself so understanding, so noble and tolerant, that you are moved by your own generosity, and she as well. "It's true I still think highly of him, but I'm sure that I couldn't have been even moderately happy with him." "Well, what makes you so sure? Didn't you say that he's a good sort?" "Of course he is. But that isn't enough. I can't even argue that he's very frivolous and I'm profound; for I'm not so deep that a good dose of frivolity would bother me, nor is he so frivolous that he is never moved by a truly deep sentiment. The difficulties were of another order. I believe that our greatest obstacle was that we didn't feel capable of communicating with each other. He exasperated me; I exasperated him. Possibly he loved me; how would one know? But the one thing certain is that he had a special flair for hurting me." How marvelous! I had to make a great effort to prevent my satisfaction from bursting out all over my face, and instead to take on the expression of someone who is really sorry that all that had to finish in frustration. I even had the strength to take my enemy's part. "And didn't you think that perhaps you too had your share of blame? Perhaps he hurt you because you were always expecting him to hurt you. To live forever on the defensive is not, I'm sure, the most effective way of creating a good life together." Then she smiled and said only, "With you it's not necessary for me to live on the defensive. And I feel happy." That put my forces of argument and dissimulation to rout. Satisfaction burst out from every pore, my smile stretched from ear to ear, and I was no longer interested in dedicating myself to ruining for good and all the surviving prestige of poor Enrique, the world's biggest loser.

Muñoz, Robledo, Méndez all talked to me with insistence about Avellaneda, how well she had worked during my absence, and what a good comrade she had shown herself to be. What's going on? How did Avellaneda behave in those days so as to make those insensitive men become so emotional? Even the manager called me, and, among other matters, let fall these casual words: "How is that girl you have in your section? I hear good things about her work." I put together a measured eulogy, in the most conventional tone in the world. But the Crab added: "Do you know why I asked? Because perhaps I'll bring her in here, as secretary." I smiled mechanically. Beneath my smile there were plenty of four-letter words.

I think that in this matter we feel alike: we have an imperious need to tell everything to each other. I speak with her as if I were talking with myself; in reality, even better than if I were talking with myself. It is as if Avellaneda had become a part of my soul, as if she were nestling in a corner of my being, waiting for my confidences, demanding my sincerity. She, on her side, also tells me everything. At another time I know I would have added, "At least I think so," but now it wouldn't be applicable. Now I know that she tells me everything.

I saw Vignale in the tearoom, well hidden at a little table in the back, with a little dame who was striking enough. He greeted me with a wide gesture, as if to confirm to me that he had launched on a large-scale adventure. As I saw that pair from a distance they gave me something to worry about. Suddenly I found myself thinking: "And I?" Of course, Vignale is a clumsy, inflated, vulgar type. . . . But what about me? How would I look to someone who's regarding me from a distance? I go out very little with Avellaneda. Our life runs its course in the office and the apartment. I'm wondering if my reluctance to go out with her isn't based more than anything on a strong fear of making a bad impression on those who would see us. No, that couldn't be. In a moment when Vignale was talking to the waiter, the girl shot a hard, contemptuous glance at him. Avellaneda couldn't look at me like that.

SATURDAY, SEPTEMBER 7

Esteban's friend has made an appointment with me. It's practically sure that my retirement will be arranged to take place within four months. It's curious: the nearer my quitting comes, the more intolerable I find the office. I know that I have still only four months of entries, counter-entries, trial balances, sight drafts, sworn affidavits. But I'd give a year of my life for those four months to be reduced to zero. Well, on second thought, I wouldn't give a year of my life, for now my life belongs to Avellaneda.

SUNDAY, SEPTEMBER 8

This afternoon we made love. We've done it so many times, and still I haven't written about it. But today it was something marvelous. Never in my life, not with

Isabel or anyone else, have I felt so close to glory. At times I think that Avellaneda is like some sort of machine that has been inserted in my breast and is expanding it, and giving it the dimensions it needs to feel more deeply every day. I cetainly didn't know I held within me these reserves of tenderness. And I don't care if that word sounds sentimental. I have tenderness and I'm proud to have it. So much so that my desire becomes pure, so that the act most definitely consecrated to sex becomes almost without stain. But this purity is not prudery, it's not affectation, it's not pretending that only the soul is involved. This purity means loving every inch of her skin, it means breathing her odor, it means caressing her belly, pore by pore.

MONDAY, SEPTEMBER 9

In the Sales Department they have prepared a terrific joke on one Menéndez, a naïve, superstitious, intense boy, who came into the firm as part of the same group as Santini, Sierra and Avellaneda. It turns out that Menéndez has bought a full ticket for tomorrow's lottery. He said that this time he wasn't going to show it to anyone, because he had the presentiment that if he didn't show it, his number would come up as the big winner. But this afternoon the collector came from Penarol, and Menéndez, as he opened his wallet to pay him, left the number on the counter for a few seconds. He didn't notice it, but Rosas, an idiot who lets nothing get by him, made a mental note of the number and immediately spread it around by word of mouth. The gag they've prepared for tomorrow is as follows: They have arranged with the lottery office opposite us that, at a fixed time, they will display on the blackboard No.

15301 where the first prize is shown. Only for a few minutes, then they'll rub it out. At the lottery shop they were so tickled by the idea of the joke that, contrary to expectations, they agreed to collaborate.

TUESDAY, SEPTEMBER 10

It was tremendous—at least to begin with. At two-forty-five Gaizolo came from the street and said in a loud voice, "God damn it to hell! I had been playing number one until last Saturday, and it just comes up today." From the rear came the first question we anticipated: "So it ended in one. Do you remember the last two numbers?" "Zero one," was the ill-humored reply. Then Pena jumped from his desk. "Hey, I played three-o-one," and he added right away, turning to Menéndez, who worked in front of the window, "Get busy, Menéndez, keep an eye on the blackboard. If three-o-one comes up I'll be really rich." It seems that Menéndez turned his head with much restraint, in the attitude of a man who's making a great effort not to have false hopes. He saw the large and clear digits of 15301 and for a moment he sat as if paralyzed. I think that in that one instant he had weighed all the possibilities and had rejected any possible trick. No one, save himself, knew the number. But the joke was supposed to stop there. The plan had been that, at that moment, the whole gang would come up, tell him what was what, and have a big laugh. But nobody had foreseen that Menéndez would make a leap and would exit running by the rear. The version of one witness is that he burst without knocking into the manager's office (who at that moment was taking care of a representative of an American firm), practically dragged him upright, and before he could give expression to his astonishment Menéndez had imprinted a resounding kiss on his bald spot. I had become aware of this latest turn of events, so I came in behind him on the run, took him by the arm and pulled him out by main force. There, among the cases of bolts and pistons, while he burst out into peals of maniacal laughter which I shall never be able to forget, I practically yelled the real truth at him. I felt horrible doing that, but I had no other recourse. I never saw a man collapse in so sudden and irreparable a manner. His legs buckled under him, he opened his mouth without being able to close it, and then—only then—he covered his eyes with his hand. I sat him down in a chair and went into the manager's office to explain the episode, but that other idiot couldn't get over the fact that the American representative had witnessed his humiliation. "Don't wear yourself out trying to explain an incredible story. That imbecile is fired."

That's the horrible part; he's really discharged, and undoubtedly embittered for life. Those five minutes of frenzied illusion will never be effaced. When the others knew about his discharge they went in a body to the manager's office, but the Crab proved inflexible. This must be the saddest, most vulgar, most depressing day in all the years that I've spent at the office. However, at the end, the confraternity made a gesture: as long as Menéndez doesn't find another job, they agreed to contribute a small percentage each to make up his salary and give it to him. He still doesn't want to talk with anyone in the office. Poor guy. I'm reproaching myself for not having warned him yesterday or today. But no one could have imagined that his reaction would have been so explosive.

The day after tomorrow will be my birthday, but she showed me her gifts in advance. First she gave me the gold watch. Poor little thing. It must have used up all her savings. Then, a little embarrassed, she opened a small box and showed me her other offering: a little spiral seashell, with perfect lines. "I found it on the beach at La Paloma on my ninth birthday. A wave came in and left it at my feet, as if the sea was making me a present. I believe it was the happiest moment of my childhood. In any case it's the material object I love and admire the most. I want you to have it and to carry it with you. Does that seem ridiculous?" Right now it's in the palm of my hand. We are going to be good friends.

Diego is a worried man, and thanks to his influence Blanca has been converted into another worrier. This evening I had a long talk with the two of them. Their worry is about the country, their own generation and, at the bottom of both abstractions, their worry is named Themselves. Diego wants to do something rebellious, positive, stimulating, renovating; he doesn't quite know what. Up to now what he has felt most intensely is an aggressive nonconformism, which lacks a bit in coherence. To him the apathy of us people seems sad, as does our lack of social impulse, our democratic tolerance that extends even to fraud, our dull and listless reaction to being deceived. It seems terrible to him, for example, that there should exist a morning paper with sixteen editorial writers who write for a hobby, sixteen capitalists who from their bungalows at Punta del Este declaim against this horrible resort where they bathe and relax, sixteen "father's boys" who use all their intelligence, all their powers of expression, to develop with skillful pervasiveness a theme in which they don't believe, a diatribe which they themselves consider unjust. It angers him that even the leftists accept for themselves, without hiding it very much, a substructure of bourgeois comfort, of rigid conventions, of hypocritical moderation. "Do you see any way out?" he asks again and again, with a frank and provocative anxiety. "For my part I don't see any. There are people who understand what is going on, who think it all absurd, but they limit themselves to deploring it. Passion is lacking—that's the secret of this great democratic mess into which we've converted ourselves. During the past decades we have been tranquil and objective; but objectivity is too inoffensive, it doesn't serve to change the world— even a pocket country like ours. We need passion, clamorous passion, clamorously felt, clamorously expressed. It has to be shouted into people's ears, since their apparent deafness is a sort of self-defense, a cowardly and unhealthy self-defense. We must succeed in awakening in the rest of the crowd an ashamedness of themselves, so that instead of self-defense they'll have self-disgust. The day that the Uruguayan will feel disgust for his own passivity, that day he'll be changed into something useful."

FRIDAY, SEPTEMBER 13

I've completed fifty years of life. That means that from today I'm eligible for retirement. A date that seems picked out for a self-review. But I've been taking off that kind of trial balance all the year. I'm annoyed by anniversaries, the idea of having joys and sorrows at fixed dates. It seems depressing to me, for example, that on the second of November we are supposed to weep in chorus over our departed ones, and that on August 25 we must excite ourselves at the view of our national flag. It's either so, or it isn't so; the day makes no difference.

SATURDAY, SEPTEMBER 14

However, yesterday's date didn't go by in vain. Today, at various times of the day, I thought: "Fifty years," and my heart dropped to my boots. I stood before the mirror, and I couldn't escape a bit of pity, a little commiseration, toward that wrinkled fellow, with tired eyes, who never got and never will get anywhere. The most tragic fate is not to be mediocre and unconscious of one's mediocrity. What's really most tragic is to be mediocre and to know it, but not to accept that destiny, which, on the other hand (that's the worst), is a strictly just one. Then, while I was contemplating myself in the mirror, there appeared over my shoulder the head of Avellaneda. This wrinkled chap, who never got and never will get anywhere, found his eyes lighting up, and for two hours and a half he forgot that he was fifty years old.

SUNDAY, SEPTEMBER 15

She laughs. I ask her, "Do you realize what fifty years mean?" and she laughs. But perhaps at bottom she does realize everything, and is placing many different thoughts in the balance. However, she's kind and says nothing about it to me. She doesn't mention that there will come the inevitable moment when I shall look at her without thinking of sex, when her hand in my hand will not be an electric shock, when I shall maintain for her the sweet affection that one has for nieces, the daughters of friends, far-away film actresses—an affection that is a kind of mental ornament because it lacks the power to wound or be wounded, it can't leave scars or wear out the heart—a soft, peaceful, harmless affection, that appears as a preview of the monotonous love of God. Then I shall look at her and shan't be able to feel jealousy, for I shall have passed the period of storms. When in the clear sky of the sixties a cloud appears, one knows it is the cloud of death. This should be the most pretentious, the most ridiculous sentence that I've entered into this notebook. But perhaps the truest. Why should it be that the truth always sounds a little ridiculous? In our thoughts we try to construct systems full of dignity and excellence, but excuses, twistings and reservations are nestled in reality, and when we get to the real they disarm and weaken us. The more worthy the proposals to be accomplished, the more ridiculous appear those we have failed to accomplish. I shall look at her, and shan't be able to feel jealous of anyone; only jealous of myself, of that individual who today feels jealous of everybody.

I went out with Avellaneda and with my fifty years; I walked with her and them all along Eighteenth Street. I wanted people to see me with her. I believe that I didn't pass anyone of the office. But I was seen by Vignale's wife, a friend of Jaime and two of Avellaneda's family. Furthermore (what a horrible "furthermore"), on Eighteenth and Yaguarón, Isabel's mother went by. It's unbelievable; years and years have passed over my face and hers, and yet when I see her my heart gives a turn. It's really more than a turn, it's a whole leap of rage and impotence. An invincible woman, so invincible that one can't do less than take off one's hat to her. She greeted me with the same aggressive reticence of twenty years ago, and then literally wrapped up Avellaneda in a long scrutiny, which at the same time diagnosed and disposed of her. Avellaneda perceived the shock I had, squeezed my arm and asked me who it was. "My mother-in-law," I said. And that's correct; my first and only mother-in-law. For even if I had never been Isabel's husband, this most high, potent and decisive matron of seventy years would from always and for always have been my universal mother-in-law, the inescapable, the destined one, my mother-in-law who proceeds directly from that God of terror who—God grant!—doesn't exist; even if it were only to remind me that the world is like that, that the world stops at times to contemplate us, with a look that, like hers, can manage to diagnose and dispose of us in one fell swoop.

MONDAY, SEPTEMBER 16

We left the office practically together, but she didn't want to go to the apartment. She's caught a cold. So we went to the pharmacy and I bought her some cough syrup. Then we took a taxi and I left her two blocks from her house. I don't want to run the risk of her father's learning about us. She walked a few steps, turned around and gave me a cheerful wave of her hand. At bottom nothing in that was so important. But there was familiarity and simplicity in the gesture. At that instant I was moved; I could not doubt that between her and me there exists a communication, with some limitations, perhaps, but right now serene and certain.

TUESDAY, SEPTEMBER 17

Avellaneda didn't come to the office.

WEDNESDAY, SEPTEMBER 18

Santini started his confidences again. He's revolting, but at the same time he's amusing. He says that his sister doesn't do any more nude dancing. She has a sweetheart.

Avellaneda didn't come today, either. It seems that her mother telephoned while I was out, and spoke with Muñoz. She says her daughter has the grippe.

THURSDAY, SEPTEMBER 19

Today I really began to miss her. They were talking about her in the section, and suddenly I couldn't stand the fact that she hadn't come.

FRIDAY, SEPTEMBER 20

Avellaneda didn't come today, either. This afternoon I was in the apartment, and in five minutes everything became clear to me. In five minutes all my scruples disappeared: I'm going to get married. More than all the arguments I have been making, more than all my conversations with her, more than all that—the thing that counts is her absence. How I've grown used to her, to her presence!

SATURDAY, SEPTEMBER 21

I confessed my intentions to Blanca, and made her happy. I must tell them to Avellaneda, I must indeed, because now I've found all strength and all conviction. But she didn't come today either.

SUNDAY, SEPTEMBER 22

Couldn't she send me a telegram? She has forbidden me to go to her house, but if she doesn't appear on Monday, in some fashion, I'll find a pretext to visit her.

MONDAY, SEPTEMBER 23

My God. My God. My God. My God. My God. My God.

FRIDAY, JANUARY 17

It's almost four months that I have made no entries. On September 23 I didn't have the strength to write what happened.

On September 23, at three in the afternoon, the telephone rang. Surrounded by employees, forms, requests, I picked up the receiver. A man's voice said, "Señor Santomé? Listen, you're speaking with an uncle of Laura. Bad news, sir. Very, very bad news. Laura passed away this morning."

In the first moment I didn't want to understand. Laura wasn't anyone; she wasn't Avellaneda. "She passed away," said the uncle's voice. The expression is loathsome. "Passed away" signifies formalities. "Bad news," the uncle had said. What does he know? Who knows how bad news can destroy the future, the countenance, the touch, the dream? Who knows, eh? The only thing he knows is to say, "She passed away," something as intolerably easy as that. Without question he was shrugging his shoulders. And that too was loathsome. It was for that reason that I committed a horrible act. With my left hand I rolled a sales list into a ball; with my right hand I brought the phone to my mouth and said slowly, "Why don't you go to the devil?" I don't remember very well. I think the voice asked several times, "What's that you say, sir?" but I also said several times, "Why don't you go to the devil?" Then they took the instrument from me and spoke with the uncle. I think I yelled my head off and said crazy things. I could hardly breathe. I felt that they opened up my collar and loosened my necktie. An unknown voice said, "It's been an emotional shock," and another voice which I really knew, that of Muñoz, started to explain: "It was an employee whom he appreciated greatly." In that cloud of sounds there were also sobs by Santini, a very low-level explanation by Robledo of the mystery of death, and the ritual orders of the manager to send a wreath. At the end, between Sierra and Muñoz, they got me into a taxi and brought me home.

Blanca opened the door, scared to death, but Muñoz calmed her right away: "Don't worry, señorita, your father is all right. Do you know what happened? One of our co-workers passed away and he was greatly affected. And with good reason, for she was a tremendous girl." He too said "passed away." OK; perhaps the uncle, Muñoz and the others did well to say "passed away," because that sounds so ridiculous, so cold, so far from Avellaneda that it can't hurt her, it can't destroy her.

Then, when I was home, alone in my room, when even poor Blanca had withdrawn the comfort of her silence, I moved my lips to say, "She died. Avellaneda died," for "died" is the word, "died" is the collapse of life, "died" comes from within, it carries the true breath of grief; "died" is disappearance, total and frigid nothingness, the simple abyss, the abyss. Then, when I moved my lips to say, "She died," then I saw my dreadful aloneness, that which was left of me, and it was very little. With all the selfishness at my command I thought about myself, about the agonized piece of patchwork that now I had become. But that was, in turn, the most generous way of thinking of her, of imagining her to the fullest. For up to 3 P.M. of September 23 I had much more of Avellaneda in me than I had of myself. She had begun to enter inside of me, to convert herself into me, like a river which is mixed too much with the sea and in the end becomes salty as the sea. Therefore, when I moved my lips and said, "She died," I felt transfixed, despoiled, empty, without value. Somebody had come and decreed: "Let them rob this fellow of four-fifths of his being." And they have despoiled me. The worst of all is that this remnant which now is me, that fifth part of myself into which they have changed me, remains quite conscious of its paucity, its insignificance. They have left me only a fifth part of my good propositions, my good projects, my good intentions, but the fifth part of my intelligence that is left is enough to make me realize that what remains won't help me. The thing is finished, and that's all.

I didn't want to go to her house, I didn't want to see her

dead, because that would be an indecent thing. That I should see her, and she not see me. That I should touch her, and she not touch me. That I should live and she not live. She is something else than that; she is our last day; like that I can treat her as equal to equal. She is the one getting out of the taxi, with the remedy I had bought for her; she is the one walking a few steps and turning around to wave to me. The last, last, last gesture. I cry, and I cling to it. On that day I wrote of my secure feeling that a complete communication existed between her and me. But the security existed while she existed. Now my lips move to say, "She died. Avellaneda died," and the security has become valueless, shameless; it is an indecent thing, that has nothing to do here. I went back to the office, of course, where the comments struck at me, annoyed me, made me feel sick. "Her cousin told me that it was a common, ordinary grippe, and suddenly—bang!—she has heart failure." I got back once more into the work, I disposed of matters, got rid of questioners, prepared requested information. Truly I am an exemplary official. At times Muñoz or Robledo or even Santini come up to me and try to start an evocative conversation with preliminaries of this type: "To think that Avellaneda used to do this work"; "Look, chief, this annotation is by Avellaneda." Then I turn my eyes away and say, "Well, it's all right, but I have to keep on living." The credits I gained here on September 23 I've lost, with interest. I know that they are murmuring that I'm an egoist, an insensitive person, that other people's misfortunes don't touch me. I don't care if they murmur. They were outside. Outside of that world in which Avellaneda and I existed. Outside of that world in which I now exist, alone like a hero, but with no reason to feel courageous.

At times I speak of her with Blanca. I don't cry; I don't give way to despair; I speak simply. I know there's an echo here. It is Blanca who cries, she who despairs. She says she can't believe in God. God had been giving me my opportunities and taking them away, and she hasn't the strength to believe in a God of cruelty, who is a sadist in every way. However, I don't feel so full of rancor. On September 23 I not only wrote many times: "My God." I said it out loud too. I felt it. For the first time in my life I felt that I could talk with him. But in the dialogue God took a weak and vacillating part, as if he were not too sure of himself. Perhaps I was at the point of affecting him. I had the sensation, furthermore, of possessing a decisive argument which was next to me, right in front of me, but which, in spite of that, I couldn't recognize and incorporate in my allegations. Then, when the period he had given me for convincing him had passed, and the indications of vacillation and weakness had passed as well, then God finally regained his forces. God became once more the all-powerful Negation that he always was. However, I can't hold a grudge against him, I can't touch and feel him with my hate. I know that he gave me the opportunity, and I didn't know how to make the best of it. Perhaps someday I'll be able to take hold of that unique and decisive argument, but when that "someday" arrives I'll be frightfully worn out, and this present relationship still more worn out. At times I think that if God played the game fairly he would also have given me the argument that I should have used against him. But no. That can't be. I don't want a God who would baby me, who would not turn over to me the key by which I may return, sooner or later, to my own conscience; I don't want a God who gives me everything ready-made, as one of those prosperous fathers of the Rembla, rotten rich, will do for his good-for-nothing and useless little son. Not that. Now the relations between God and me have chilled. He knows that I'm not capable of convincing him. I know that he is a distant solitude, to which I've never had and never will have access. Thus we remain, each of us on his own ground, not hostile, not loving, just strange to one another.

FRIDAY, JANUARY 24

Today, throughout the day, while I had breakfast, while I worked, while I lunched, while I discussed things with Muñoz, I was overshadowed by a single idea, split up in its turn into various doubts: "What was she thinking before she died? What did I represent for her at that instant? Did she turn to me? Did she say my name?"

SUNDAY, JANUARY 26

For the first time I read over my diary, from February to January. I must look for all Her Moments. She appeared on February 27. On March 12 I noted: "When she says 'Señor Santomé' she always blinks. She's not a beauty, but she smiles passably. A little something is better than nothing." I wrote that. There was a time when I thought that of her. On April 10: "Avellaneda has something that attracts me. That's evident, but what is it?" Well, what was it? I still don't know. What attracted me were her eyes, her voice, her waist, her mouth, her hands, her laugh, her being tired, her bashfulness, her tears, her frankness, her sorrow, her confidence, her tenderness, her dreams, her step, her sighs. But none of those traits was sufficient to attract me compulsively and totally. Each attraction was supported by another. She attracted me as a whole, as an unsubstitutable sum of attractions each of which might have been substitutable. On May 17 I said, "I think I'm in love with you," and she answered, "I knew that." She still is saying that, I hear her saying it, and all this present becomes unbearable. Two days later: "what I am seeking can be termed an accord, a kind of compromise between my love and your liberty." She had replied, "I like you." It's horrible how those three words hurt me now. On June 7 I kissed her, and that night I wrote: "Tomorrow I'll think about that. Now I'm tired. But I can also write: happy. Yet I'm too much on guard to call myself totally happy. On guard against myself, against fortune, against that only tangible future, which is called 'tomorrow.' On guard; that is to say suspicious." However, what good was that suspiciousness to me? Did I perchance make use of it to live more intensely, more passionately, more peremptorily? Certainly not. Afterward I acquired a certain sense of security, I thought that everything was all right if one was conscious of loving, and of loving with an echo, a repercussion. On June 23 she spoke to me of her parents, of the theory of happiness invented by her mother. Perhaps I should do something to get to know her mother. Perhaps I should replace my inexorable universal mother-in-law with that good image, with that woman who understands and pardons. On June 28 took place the most important event in my life. I— of all people—finished by praying, "May it only last"; and to bring pressure on God I touched the right kind of wood.

But God turned out to be incorruptible. Still, on July 6 I allowed myself to note down: "All at once I realized that this moment, this tiny slice of daily life, was the culmination of well-being; it was happiness." But right away I gave myself a warning slap: "I am sure that the summit of happiness lasts only a second, a short second, a momentary illumination, and no one has the right to prolong it." I wrote that without meaning it, however; now I know it's true. For at bottom I had faith that there would be a continuation, that the summit was not only a point, but a wide, infinite plane. But it had no right to continue, of course not. Afterward I wrote about the word "Avellaneda," and all the meanings that it held. Now I think "Avellaneda" and the word means, "She doesn't exist, she will never exist again." I can't go on.

TUESDAY, JANUARY 28

In my notebook there are so many other things, so many other faces: Vignale, Aníbal, my children, Isabel. None of that is important, none of that exists now. While Avellaneda was here, I understood better Isabel's epoch and Isabel herself. But now Avellaneda isn't here, and Isabel has disappeared behind a thick and dark metal curtain, the kind one pulls down before a store window.

FRIDAY, JANUARY 31

At the office I defend tenaciously that part of my life (my death) which is essential, innermost, profound. No one knows exactly what is going on inside me. My collapse of September 23 was, for everybody, an understandable upset, and nothing more. Now they are talking less about Avellaneda, and I don't bring up the subject. I defend her with my poor strength.

MONDAY, FEBRUARY 3

She gave me her hand, and I didn't need anything else. That was enough to make me feel that I was welcome. More than my kissing her, more than our sleeping together, she gave me her hand, and that was love.

THURSDAY, FEBRUARY 6

The idea came to me the other night, and today I carried it out. At five o'clock I dashed from the office. When I came to No. 368 and rang the bell I felt an itching in my throat and I began to cough.

The door opened while I was coughing like a condemned man. It was her father, the same father as in the photos, but older, sadder, more fatigued. I coughed even harder, but at last I overcame the spasm and succeeded in asking if he was the tailor. He bent his head to one side to answer yes. "Good, I wanted to order a suit." He led me into his workshop. ("Never go to him for a suit," Avellaneda had said. "He makes them all to fit the same manikin.") There it was—imperturbable, comical, castrated—the manikin. I picked out the cloth, specified some details, agreed on the price. Then he went over to the back door and called, without shouting, "Rosa." ("Mother knows about Our Matter," she had said. "My mother knows everything about me.") But Our Matter didn't include my name, my face, my stature. For her mother Our Matter was Avellaneda and a lover without a name. "My wife," said the father, presenting her. "Señor—what did you say was your name?" "Morales," I lied. "Of course; Señor Morales." The mother's eyes held a penetrating sadness. "He's getting a suit made." Neither of the two was wearing mourning. Their grief was unforced and natural. The mother smiled at me. I had to look toward the manikin, for it was beyond my strength to endure that smile that had been Avellaneda's smile. The father opened a small book and began to take my measurements, dictating two-digit numbers. "Are you of this district? Seventy-five." I said, "More or less." "I ask you that because I seem to know your face. Fifty-four." "Well, I live in the Center, but I often come this way." "Oh, that's it. Sixty-nine." She took it down automatically, looking at the wall. "You want the trousers to fall on the shoe, don't you? One-o-six."

I have to come back next Thursday, to try it on. There was a book on the table: Blavatsky. He had to leave for a moment. The mother closed the little book and looked at me. "What made you decide to have my husband make you a suit? Who recommended him?" "Oh, no one especially. I was informed that a tailor lived here, that's all." That sounded so unconvincing that I was ashamed. She looked at me again. "Now he works very little. Since our daughter died." She did not say "passed away." "Oh, of course," I remarked, although the connection wasn't clear at all. "Was it long ago?" "About four months." "I'm sorry, madam," I said, and I, who feel it not really as a grief, but as a catastrophe, a collapse, a chaos, was conscious of the lie I spoke; for to say, "I'm sorry," to pronounce that condolence, so frivolous, so delayed, was simply frightful, above all because I said it to the only person who could understand the other language, who could understand the truth.

It was the day for the fitting, but the tailor wasn't there. "Señor Avellaneda isn't here." His wife told me that when I came in. "He couldn't wait for you, but he left everything ready so that I can try it on you." She went into the other room and reappeared with the jacket. I felt awful. It was a fact after all that he made his suits to the manikin's measure. All at once I turned to one side (in reality she made me turn with the excuse of having to put in pins and make chalk marks), and I found myself in front of a photograph of Avellaneda that wasn't there last Thursday. The blow was too sudden, too brutal. Her mother was observing me and her eyes took good note of my surprise and the havoc it made. Then she put the remaining pins and the chalk on the table and smiled sadly, now quite sure, before asking me, "You . . . are?" Between the first and the second words there was a blank space of two or three seconds, but this silence was enough to convert the question into something transparent. I had to reply. And I answered without saying a word; with my head, with my eyes, with all my being I said, "Yes." Avellaneda's mother rested her hand on my arm, on the arm that, still minus a sleeve, emerged from that awkwardly made confection in its basting threads. Then she slowly removed the jacket and placed it over the manikin. How well it fitted there. "You want to know, don't you?" I am sure that she was not looking at me with bitterness, or with shame, or with anything one could call pity. "You knew her, you loved her, and you are suffering. I know how you feel. You feel that your heart is an enormous thing that begins in your stomach and finishes in your throat. You feel unhappy, and happy to be unhappy. I know how horrible that is." She was speaking as if she had met again with an old-time confidant, but still she was speaking with something more than her present grief. "Twenty years ago someone died to me. Someone who was everything. But he didn't die this kind of death. He just went away. Out of the country, out of my life, above all out of my life. That death was worse, I can assure you. For it was I who asked him to go away, and I have never forgiven myself since. That death is worse, because one remains imprisoned in one's own past, destroyed by one's own sacrifice." She passed her hand over the back of her neck, and I thought she was about to say: "I don't know why I'm telling these things to you." But, instead, she added, "Laura was the last thing of his that remained to me. That's why I feel for a second time that my heart is an enormous thing that begins in my stomach and ends in my throat. That's why I know what is going on inside you." She brought up a chair and sank into it, exhausted. I asked, "And she, what did she know of that?" "Nothing," she said. "Laura knew absolutely nothing. I was the only one who knew my story. A poor sort of pride, wasn't it?" Suddenly I remembered. "And your theory of happiness?" "She told you that too? It was a lovely lie, a fairy tale so that my daughter would not lose courage, so that she could feel that she was really living. It was the best present I ever made her." Poor little woman. She was weeping with her head held high, without shielding her eyes; she was crying proudly. "But you want to know," she said. Then she told me of the last days, the last moments, the last words of Avellaneda. But that I shall never put down. That is mine, incorruptibly mine. That will be waiting for me at night, every night, whenever I shall take up again the thread of my sleeplessness, and say, "Love."

FRIDAY, FEBRUARY 14

"They love each other, I'm sure of that," Avellaneda used to say about her parents, "but I don't know if I like that way of loving."

SATURDAY, FEBRUARY 15

Esteban's friend telephoned to advise me that my retirement is now ready. After the first of March I won't be going to the office.

SUNDAY, FEBRUARY 16

I went for my suit this morning. Señor Avellaneda was about through with ironing it. The photo filled the room, and I couldn't stop looking at it. "That is my daughter," he said, "my only daughter." I don't know what I answered, and I don't want to remember. "She died a short time ago." Once more I heard myself reciting, "I'm sorry." "It's a strange thing," he added. "Now I think I was too distant, and I never showed her how much I needed her. Ever since she was a child I kept postponing the long conversation I had promised myself I would have with her. First I didn't have time; then she began to work; and, besides, I am pretty much of a coward. I was a bit scared, you know, about feeling sentimental. Now she is gone, and I'm left with that charge in my heart, with those unborn words that could have been my salvation." He stopped speaking for a moment and contemplated the photo. "Many times I thought that she hadn't inherited a single one of my features. Do you find any?" "In a general way," I lied. "That could be," said he. "But in her soul she was like me. I should say, like I was. But now I feel defeated, and when one lets oneself be defeated, one becomes deformed and converted into a gross parody of oneself. Look, that death of my daughter was a dirty trick. Of fate, or of the doctor, I don't really know which. But I'm sure that it was a dirty trick. If you had known her you'd understand what I'm trying to tell you." I blinked my eyes some ten times in a row, but he paid no attention. "Only by a dirty trick could they destroy a girl like that. She was—how can I explain it?—a clear, transparent being, and at the same time intense, and at the same time powerful in her intensity. She was an enchantment. I was always convinced that I didn't deserve that daughter. Her mother, Rosa, did deserve her, for Rosa has character, she is capable of confronting the world. But I lack decisiveness; I'm not sure of myself. Did you ever think of committing suicide? I have. But I'll never be able to. And that also is a failing. For I have the complete mental and moral pattern of the suicide, save for the strength needed to put a bullet through my temple. Perhaps that is because my brain has some of the needs of my heart and my heart has some of the needs of my brain." Once again he became immobile, this time with the iron in the air, looking at the photo. "Notice her eyes. Notice how their gaze continues, even more than it did in life, and in spite of her death. She seems even to be looking at *you*." The sentence had no successor, for I had no breath to speak, and he was left with nothing to add. "Well, it's ready now," he said, carefully folding the trousers. "It's a good, carded cloth. See how well it took the iron."

TUESDAY, FEBRUARY 18

I shan't go to 368. Really, I just can't go there anymore.

THURSDAY, FEBRUARY 20

I haven't seen Aníbal for a long time. I don't know anything about Jaime. Esteban limits himself to speaking with me about general subjects. Vignale calls me at the office, and I tell them to say I'm not there. I want to be alone. At most, to talk with my daughter. And to speak of Avellaneda, of course.

SUNDAY, FEBRUARY 23

Today, after four months, I was in the apartment. I opened the clothes closet. Her perfume was there. It didn't help. What counts is her absence. Her absence was here today. Under some circumstances I can't quite get the nuances which separate inertia from desperation.

MONDAY, FEBRUARY 24

It's evident that God has granted me an obscure destiny. Not even a cruel one, just obscure. It's evident that he granted me a truce. At the beginning I struggled against believing that it could be happiness. I resisted with

all my strength; afterward I acknowledged myself van-
quished and I believed. But it wasn't happiness, it was
only a truce. Now once more I am swallowed up in my
destiny. And it's more obscure than before, much more.

TUESDAY, FEBRUARY 25

After March 1 I won't pick up this notebook
again. The world has lost its interest. I won't be the one
who sets down that fact. There's only one theme I could
write about. And I don't want to.

WEDNESDAY, FEBRUARY 26

How I need her. God has been my most important
need. But I need her more than God.

THURSDAY, FEBRUARY 27

They wanted to give me a farewell party at the
office, but I refused. In order not to appear ill-mannered I
offered a persuasive excuse based on family problems. The
truth is that I can't imagine myself the savorless subject of
a joyous, noisy dinner, with bread being thrown around and
wine spilled on the table.

FRIDAY, FEBRUARY 28

The last day of work. No work done, of course.
I spent it shaking hands and receiving embraces. I believe
that the manager was overflowing with satisfaction and
that Muñoz was really touched. My table will stay there.

[183]

I never thought that I would care so little about giving up my routine. I emptied out the drawers. In one of them I found an identification card of Avellaneda. She had left it with me so we could register the number in her personnel file. I put it in my pocket, and it's there now. The photo must be about five years old, but four months ago she was prettier. One other thing is now clear, and that is that her mother was wrong: I don't feel happy about feeling unhappy. I simply feel unhappy. I'm finished with the office. Beginning tomorrow, and up to the day of my death, my time will be at my disposal. After waiting so long, this is leisure. What shall I do with it?

Montevideo,
January to May, 1959